THE GREEN CLASSROOM

"We did not inherit the land from our forefathers,
we hold it in trust for our children."

Chief Seattle

Adrienne Mason

THE GREEN CLASSROOM

101 practical ways to involve students in environmental issues

Foreword by Janet E. Grant

Pembroke Publishers Limited

I would like to thank Jill Fenton and Anne Landry for their constant encouragement, support, and faith in my abilities, the staff and students of Jasper Elementary School for their ideas and resources, and Bob — who else would have put up with so much and lived to tell the tale?

Adrienne Mason

© 1991 Pembroke Publishers Limited
528 Hood Road
Markham, Ontario
L3R 3K9

Canadian Cataloguing in Publication Data
Mason, Adrienne
 The green classroom

Includes index.
ISBN 0-921217-60-9

1. Environmental protection — Study and teaching (Elementary). 2. Activity programs in education. 3. Creative activities and seat work. I. Title.

TD170.6.M38 1991   372.3'5   C91-093238-7

Editor: Lou Pamenter
Design: John Zehethofer
Cover Art: Phyllis Wong Kun

Printed and bound in Canada
9 8 7 6 5 4 3 2

Strategies for involving students in environmental issues

In this age of environmental concern, teachers and the children in their classrooms are being asked to take a leading role in saving the environment. For teachers the challenge of teaching the environment is two-fold: to find stimulating activities that enable students to explore the background behind various environmental issues, and to structure activities so that students understand that taking care of the environment is a natural part of their day-to-day existence — just like going to school, doing homework, and playing with their friends.

One way of motivating students to become involved in the environment is to use their natural interests and skills. Given the opportunity to use their own interests and skills, students can come up with the most amazing ideas about how they would like to save the environment. As the students watch their ideas grow and solve real issues, they may demonstrate new self-confidence or even turn their ideas into volunteer work. (Their enthusiasm is definitely linked to the fact that the environment is one of the few places where age is no barrier.)

The following exercise can be used by teachers as a starter for finding out what the students naturally turn to. Teachers should work through the exercise themselves first to understand the sort of thinking required and the decisions being made at each stage. For example, the environmental issue about which you feel most strongly may change as you discover new information about other environmental issues. Share your own anecdotes about how you made your choice.

What Is Most Important to You? (Step #1 of the Kid's Green Plan)

My Green Plan   *My Name*   *Date*

The environment issue I find the most interesting is: ....

My favourite interest or hobby is: ....

I am most skilled at: ....

Ask your class which issue is most important to them, e.g. wildlife, water, forests, garbage. It's great if the students have some background on environmental issues before they make a choice, but it is not mandatory. They will choose issues for all sorts of different reasons. Students may select an issue because of one of the following factors:

(1) "It's a local issue." Their parents' cottage or home is on a lake that is experiencing a loss in its loon or fish population due to acid rain or they live in a community where forests are being threatened or they live in a province where industry's need for more water is prompting the building of dams which disturb forests and their wildlife.

(2) "I have an interest in it." Some students may be naturally drawn to water, animals, paper and trees, or saving resources. For example, one student may be fascinated by turtles and therefore committed to doing something to save the Leatherback Turtle. Another student may be fascinated by water, and be committed to doing studies with a chemistry set on rainfall. The possibilities are as endless as the number of individuals in your classroom!

(3) "I have a skill that would be perfect for it." Students may have a drawing talent or be able to make objects with their hands, e.g. carpentry, origami, baking.

Note: Students will likely work on several different issues during the year.

Next, students choose a favourite interest or hobby and one of their best skills. Then they merge their answers together into a "green plan" they would enjoy doing. Here are just a few of the "green plans" that one group of students developed in a single classroom period. (The first line reflects the answers to the three questions in Step #1 of the Kids' Green Plan — Issue, Hobby/Interest, Skill.)

Wildlife   Shopping   Sports

Make a t-shirt about wildlife and use it in sports, and with the money you could help the wildlife and save some lives.
  This is the way the student showed the above:

KIDS GREENPLAN

forenst
water
gargage
✓ wildlife
✓ shopping

KIDS GREENPLAN

① Wildlife ② Shopping ③ Sports

You make a T-shirt or a sweetshirt about the wildlife and you could use it in sports and with the money you could help the wildlife and the enviroment. Then you might save some lifes.

Vanessa
Stewart
Nov 7/1990

Forests   Collecting baseball cards   Geography

Make baseball cards with directions to forests that need saving on the back of the cards.

Garbage   Sports   Drawing

Draw a poster of Teenage Mutant Ninja Turtles discussing the environment.

Wildlife   Hockey   Writing

Write a script about hockey and an animal.

Water   Fashion   Swimming

If I swim, I will have to care about water. I'll design a bathing suit that says, "Save the Water".

Here is another graphic example of what the students produced:

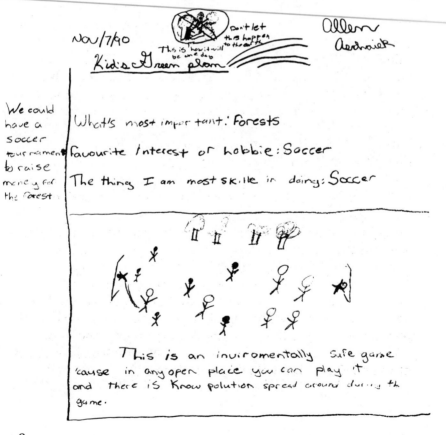

Of course, you may get plans like the following: "I would dance all over the world and raise money". A plan that for the moment obviously needs a local focus. But, who knows, that child may grow up and do exactly that!

What Is Most Important to You and The Green Classroom

Together, the "What is important to you?" exercise and the more than one hundred activities in *The Green Classroom* will provide you with enough fuel to develop exciting lesson plans over the school year. Here are four suggestions for bringing together a highly motivated "green classroom".

(1) Set up the classroom in groups according to the favourite issue. Each of the "issue" groups can be assigned a particular part of the classroom to use for its exhibits. There would be designated areas for the issues of wastes, habitats and wildlife, and rain, air, water, and energy.

(2) Set up the classroom in "favourite interest or hobby" or "skills" groups. Students who enjoy camping and fishing could participate in "A home for wildlife". Students who know everything about the newest cars might enjoy "Alternative autos". Anyone who collects hockey or baseball cards could become involved with the role-play cards used in "There's more than one answer". If students express an interest in recycling, that group can make paper from the instructions given in "Recycle a tree". Students with musical abilities could put together an orchestra of instruments from "Musical recycling". If drama is the skill grouping, try "Spreading the message". A language skills group might choose "Poetry for the environment" or "The maple leaf forever?" as activities.

(3) Allow students to choose one of four activities you have pre-selected from *The Green Classroom*. One combination of activities could be "Press agent for a day", "Supermarket savvy", "Trying to grow in acid rain", and "Keeping an energy account". Such a combination allows both individual and group participation. No matter which combination of activities you choose, remember to have the students evaluate their conclusions.

(4) Put up a bulletin board for the school year which keeps track of the students' individual green plans.

Kids Who Have Found Something Special to Do

When David Suzuki was a boy, he collected insects with his father on weekend camping trips. From these trips he came home and created insect displays. John Tuzo Wilson, the discoverer of the theory of plate tectonics and first director of the Ontario Science Centre, joined a forestry party at the age of fifteen. As a teenager, Robert Bateman joined the Junior Field Naturalists' Club, and spent hours sketching and painting in the museum.

Today, young people across the continent have been coming up with their own solutions to environmental problems after many hours of hard work. Shannon Bard in Vancouver, B.C. spent over 350 hours during 1987 and 1988 on a letter and newspaper writing campaign called S.O.S. (Save Our Shores). Sandra Imbeault and Pascale Charest, two high school students in Quebec, decided to tackle the problem of disposable diapers for a Science Fair project. By the end of their research they had come up with a commercially successful formula for recycling disposable diapers.

Teachers teaching environmental concerns have already made a large contribution to the health of the planet. The challenge continues. Green classrooms may not make every child in your classroom into a famous environmentalist, but they will ensure that children will each make an unique contribution to the environment.

Janet E. Grant
author of The Kids' Green Plan,
How to write your own plan to
save the environment.

Contents

Preface

The environment is in the news. We hear how fragile our planet is, and how we must monitor its health. We are learning that we must respect the environment, and work with it instead of against it.

Today's students are very aware of environment issues. They want to know what they can do to help. I have one young friend who proudly acts as an environmental watchdog around his house; he has been known to reprimand his mother if she happened to leave the water running while brushing her teeth. Another young person rounded up a group of friends and, with placards in hand, marched to the local government office to protest the spraying of pesticides in their community. Unfortunately, it was a Saturday morning, and the office was closed. During the 1989-90 school year, the students at Jasper Elementary School chose the environment as their school theme. Over the year, the children became increasingly aware of the influence they have as individuals.

About This Book

I wrote *The Green Classroom* so that teachers would have one source where they could find both background information on environmental issues and activities that would involve their students. Each student can find out how to help, how to be part of the solution, whether by reading the hydro meter at home, cleaning up the schoolyard, making a purchase, or studying the influences of the rainforests.

The book is organized into seven units. The first unit deals with environmental awareness, an introduction to environmental concerns. The following six units deal with the key issues of waste, habitats and wildlife, acid rain, air, water, and energy. Each of these units begins with background information for the teacher. Further background information is often given within particular activities.

Altogether, there are more than 100 activities, designed to enhance the skills and abilities of your students, while developing new ones. Students will be able to work individually or in groups, and to extend programs to the school, their homes, and their communities. Any group work improves the skills of cooperation, listening, and discussing.

As well, the activities have been designed to integrate with many different curriculum areas. This means that the activities can be used throughout a school day. For example, some sample activity topics and sample skills for a few subject areas:

- science: testing for acids and bases; constructing a bug catcher (skills — observation, comparison, classifying).
- language arts: conducting interviews; writing poetry and plays; role-playing; presenting research findings to the class (skills — visualization, interpretation, description, invention, analysis).
- creative thinking: brainstorming solutions to such problems as water conservation (skills — discussion, listening, analysis, evaluation).
- consumer education: learning about advertising and packaging (skills — learning about the power of an individual in making a difference, becoming a more astute consumer).
- art and music: making conclusions about issues using artwork; making recycled instruments (skills — description, manual dexterity, group work).
- social studies: devising Earth Day celebrations (skills — application, synthesis, evaluation).
- history: studying the historical uses of rivers (skills — research, comprehension, comparison, application, analysis).
- mathematics: measuring and graphing the acidity in snow (skills — experimentation, analysis, charting, evaluation).

Working out solutions with your students, and showing them that they can influence change will give them hope for the future. I hope that *The Green Classroom* provides the resources for your students to make choices.

Adrienne Mason

Becoming aware of our environment

Igniting the spark

To activate environmental awareness in students

Here are ten simple activities to heighten children's appreciation for nature. Getting the kids out into nature is integral to fostering an environmental ethic — they must understand their connectedness to nature in order to be responsible and caring stewards of the earth.

1. Create an unnature trail. On a section of trail hide 25 to 40 manufactured objects. Use anything — toys, nails, balloons, dice. Clear out your desk drawer! Camouflage some of the items well, keep others more obvious. Set a distance limit (one metre on either side to just above eye level). Challenge the students to find the objects that don't belong in nature (don't tell them how many are hidden at the beginning). You'll be amazed at how they slow down and start taking a closer look at the environment.

2. Take a nature hike. Emphasize smell, texture, sound, or shape. Before you leave on any hike have the students stand with their arms apart. Walk through the group and take items from different children (e.g. the glasses from one, a backpack from another, one shoe from yet another). Then signal that it's time to go. The children will protest. This is the time to emphasize that the forest needs all its parts

too and that nothing should be removed from it. Return the items you borrowed from the students.

3. Become wildlife detectives. Go on an animal sign walk. Look for eggs, tracks, holes in trees or in the ground, scats (pellets), piles of food, nests, etc.

4. Take a bug's eye view. On a nice day, go outside in the school yard or in a natural area nearby. Lie on your backs — enjoy the wind, clouds, trees and things above you. Then turn over on your stomach. How does it smell? What grows there? What lives there? What is the soil like?

5. Look at nature in the city. In your schoolyard and area around your school, look for evidence of nature fighting back from being paved over. Look for plants pushing up through concrete, lichen and other plants growing on buildings, flowers or other plants growing where they weren't planted. What birds and animals live in the city?

6. Study the variation in nature. Use birds as an example. How many different types of bird bills are there? Why are they so different? How many feet types are there in birds? The children will learn that beaks and feet are adapted for different food types and habitats. You could also study variation in animals, trees, or leaves.

7. Play nature charades. Students can act out things that occur in nature.

8. Be a blind artist. Students work in pairs. One student should be blindfolded while the other student draws a simple abstract design on a piece of paper. The artists should then describe their drawings to their partners who can not see it. The other students try to draw the design based on what they are being told. How well did the drawing turn out? It wasn't easy, was it? This is a good time to discuss communication skills. A lack of good communication skills is often the basis for our misunderstandings. Investigate some ways that animals communicate.

9. Take a blindfold walk. One student carefully leads another on a walk through a natural area. The sighted person should

lead the other to things to feel and smell. How did the ground feel underfoot? How did things smell? How did things feel?

10. Get old paint sample chips from a hardware store. Attach four different colors on an index card. Challenge students to match the colors on their cards with colors in nature.

Environment in the news

To have the students use various types of media to collect information on environmental topics

Divide the class into research teams and assign each group an environmental issue (e.g. acid rain, endangered species, global warming, sewage/garbage disposal, litter).

Each team must find current material on its topic from newspapers, magazines, radio and television reports. Use a scrapbook or bulletin board to keep the class or school up to date on the various topics.

Benefitting from nature

To examine some of the things that we use daily which come from the environment

Discuss how people are part of the environment. In pairs or alone, students make a collage that begins with a picture of people in the centre of the page. The people-picture is then surrounded with things that are used, eaten, or worn in everyday life. Old magazines and catalogues can be used for the illustrations. Using either symbols or words, students then classify what natural resource each item began as (e.g. wool sweater — animal, orange juice — plant, eggs — animal).

For comparison purposes ask students to make another collage to show what people put into the environment each day (e.g. garbage, car exhaust, packaging). Brainstorm ways in which we could reduce the amount of waste we put into the environment.

Brainstorming sessions work well if the class is divided into groups of six students, one of whom acts as a recorder. No value judgements are made on any suggestion; all suggestions are written down. A seemingly slight suggestion can often trigger another, stronger suggestion. Younger students benefit from brainstorming sessions but may need to do their "out-loud" thinking as a class, with you as the recorder.

Poetry for the environment

To encourage students to use poetry to express their feelings about the environment; students will learn that nature can be a source of inspiration

If possible do this activity outdoors. If you can't go outside take the students through a guided imagery. Describe a place, real or imaginary, to them. Describe how it looks, smells, and sounds.

Students can then compose poems based on the feelings they experienced either outside on their own or while listening to your description. Try haiku, diamantes, cinquains, free verse, or a group poem.

Discuss how poetry can have an effect on people. Have the students recall a story or poem that they particularly like or that they feel made an impression on them. They can write a sentence explaining why they like that poem or story.

Discuss whether they think the poems they have written would leave a special impression with other readers. Poems can be exchanged, discussed, and illustrated. The class may want to compile the poems into a booklet.

You may suggest one of the following poetic structures:

CINQUAIN: based on syllables or words; has five lines.
    line 1 — the title in two syllables or two words
    line 2 — describes the title in four syllables or words
    line 3 — describes actions in six syllables or words
    line 4 — describes feelings in eight syllables or words
    line 5 — another word(s) for the title, or one that relates to the title; two syllables or words

HAIKU: a Japanese form of poetry which consists of three lines of five, seven and five syllables respectively. These poems are unrhymed.

DIAMANTE: these poems usually deal with opposites (birth/death, forests/clearcut, beginning/end). They are shaped in the form of a diamond, using the following pattern:

noun

adjective adjective

participle participle participle

noun noun noun

participle participle participle

adjective adjective

noun

Stampin' about

To explore the ways in which society uses images of nature by studying postage stamps

Find a class, staff, or community member who collects postage stamps and make arrangements for a visit or a loan of their collection. Alternatively, have the class collect the stamps they receive on mail at home over the course of a month.

How many stamps have environmental themes? Do some countries use more environmental themes than others? Do many of the postage stamps use scenes from nature? Are there scenes of endangered wildlife or unique places? Do any of the stamps commemorate special events such as Environment Week?

Have students create their own stamp commemorating something in nature that is special to them. They can write a paragraph to accompany the stamp to explain why it is special enough that Canada Poste should print it.

Eco-quotes

To study some quotations about the environment

After reading the following quotations, students can describe in their own words the meanings of the quotations. Do the students know something about any of the people who made these statements? Students can choose one of the quotations and illustrate it, or they can create their own "quotable" saying.

"The frog does not drink up the pond in which he lives."
Indian proverb

"Think globally, act locally." *Anonymous*

"We abuse land because we regard it as a commodity belonging to us; when we see land as a community to which *we* belong, we may begin to use it with love and respect."
Aldo Leopold

"What is the use of a house if you haven't got a tolerable planet to put it on?" *Henry David Thoreau*

"Except during the nine months before he draws his first breath, no man manages his affairs as well as a tree."
George Bernard Shaw

"We have met the enemy and he is us." *Pogo*

"Speak to the earth, and it shall teach thee." *Job 12:8*

"I believe in God, only I spell it nature."
Frank Lloyd Wright

"There is nothing useless in nature, not even uselessness itself." *Montaigne*

"Never doubt that a small group of thoughtful, committed citizens can change the world: indeed, it's the only thing that ever has." *Dr. Margaret Mead*

"If you're not part of the solution, you're part of the problem." *Anonymous*

Systems study

To look at entire systems rather than just parts of them

Plant four whole bean seeds in separate containers. Plant a seed that is cut in half cross-wise and another that is cut in half length-wise in two more containers. Treat all the seeds the same and monitor their growth. Do the seeds that are cut in half grow? Why or why not?

Once the seeds that have sprouted have leaves, cut off the roots from one, the stem from another, and one leaf from another. Plant the remaining parts as best you can. Continue to water them. What happens to their growth?

Discuss the concept of entire systems. The plant and its seed is an entire system that needs all its parts to grow. This can also be demonstrated by looking at the parts of a flashlight, a car, or the human body. The environment is also a system that needs all its components to work properly. If one component is removed, the system shifts or adjusts.

Play the Web Game which demonstrates the concept of an entire ecosystem and how all parts of this system are necessary.

Web Game

Form a circle. Ask one student to name a plant that grows in your area (for example, grass). Have that student represent grass. Give that student a ball of string.

Ask the group, ''Who eats grass?'' (a rabbit) Have another student represent a rabbit. The grass passes the ball of string to the rabbit, holding on to one end.

Ask the group, ''What eats rabbits?'' (a lynx) The rabbit passes the ball to the lynx, holding on to a section of string.

Continue until all the children are joined to something else. Be sure to include the sun, water, soil, insects . . . anything present in the environment.

When all participants are connected, discuss the fact that you have created an ''ecosystem''. There are many parts in the system and they are all important.

Demonstrate this by trying to remove a part of the system. For example, say that the water has been polluted and is no longer usable. Have the student who represents water give his or her section of the string a good tug. See who feels that tug. Have all the students who felt the tug also give a tug. Everyone should eventually feel the effects of water pollution. Try other examples: remove a tree, put pesticide on the grass, contaminate the soil, have a species become extinct . . .

Pollution recognition

To be able to recognize the basic components of our environment, and how we use and misuse them

List the basic components of our natural environment (air, water, soil, plants, wildlife, people) on index cards. Divide the class into groups. Each group picks a card and works together to think of the many uses of the element chosen. (e.g. plants: food, oxygen, shade, fuel, shelter for wildlife, clothing, building materials).

The class then thinks of the major pollutants. These are written on individual cards (e.g. oil, chemicals, acid rain, smoke, litter, solid wastes, noise).

Separate the resource cards and the pollutant cards. Students draw one card from each pile and determine the ways in which that pollutant affects the resource. (e.g. if water and acid rain are drawn: acidifies water, makes it unsuitable for some life, can break the food chain, will eventually kill fish, fish-eating birds won't return to the lake . . .).

Seeking pollution solutions

To have students work as a group to identify pollution or conservation problems in their community, and to brainstorm for solutions

Have students identify the major pollution problems in their community. Examples might include: inferior sewage system, lack of wilderness, no room for landfills, air pollution, water pollution. Brainstorm for ideas to reduce the problems. Discuss with students how they might work to initiate change. Students could do one of the following:
• write a letter to the city council, MLA, MP, or local newspaper editor expressing their concerns and some possible solutions

- prepare a presentation on the problem that could be given to a local interest group or town council
- design a poster or flyer on the problem to distribute around town
- do a "mock" radio-interview on the problem
- act as reporters and take a public survey in which they could ask people such questions as "what is the most important environmental concern facing our community?", "what are you doing to help solve it?", "what do you suggest that government do to solve the problem?".

Spreading the message

Students will devise positive ways to educate others about environmental issues or things that they can do to help the environment

Discuss how environmental issues can sometimes overwhelm and depress us because it seems that we have no control over them. Do the students feel helpless sometimes? Does this mean that we don't have to do anything about the issues and problems? Discuss with the class what a 9th grader wrote:

"Not knowing is terrifying,
Knowing is terrifying
But not knowing is useless
And knowing may save us"

Discuss the axiom "ignorance is bliss". What does it mean? Why do people ignore problems? Do they really believe they don't exist? Do they have other things to worry about? Maybe they don't know the facts?

Have the students devise positive ways to share facts about the environment and to suggest simple things people can do to help. They can create a game, song, skit, or cartoon to "spread the word" in a fun, non-threatening manner.

Back to the future

To imagine what the future would be like if we ran out of a particular resource

Have the students list some natural resources and whether they are renewable or non-renewable (examples might include gas, coal, trees, meat, water).

Ask the students to imagine that they are living in the year 2050. Choose one resource from the list and ask the students to imagine that it is no longer available. What would we do without this resource? Would there be an alternative we could use? Has a new machine been invented so that we could do without the resource?

The students can describe their day in the future by making a poster, writing a story or play.

Press agent for a day

To demonstrate that personal biases and judgements are often present when reporting information

Using the following situation, have the students write a short, 2-3 paragraphs press release. The students should write the release from the perspective of one of the following:

— representative of a local environmental group
— president of the local birdwatching group
— fisherman
— public relations person for the Oily Oil Company
— mayor of Squeaky Clean Cove, B.C.

Situation: On July 23, 1989 the *S.S. Bunker Queen*, owned by the Oily Oil Company of Vancouver, B.C., was travelling south from Alaska with a full load of oil destined for Vancouver. During the evening of the 23rd, the *Bunker Queen* hit a large rock three kilometres offshore, close to the small fishing community of Squeaky Clean Cove. The rock was clearly shown on the ship's charts. The ship began to lose oil. There are rumors that the captain of the ship suffered from narcolepsy (a disease where the person has episodes of uncontrollable sleepiness), and he liked to play rock music at full volume to help him stay awake. Many of the residents including local fishermen, have been hired by the Oily Oil Company to help with the clean-up. They are being paid $15/hr. A seabird breeding area is near the site where the ship hit the rock.

Read out several of the press releases. Compare the various points of view and the different things emphasized in each press release. Were some things omitted by some people?

EXTENSIONS

• For one week, have students collect stories on environmental issues from magazines and newspapers. Collate the information they have gathered under various headings, such as the types of issues, the people involved, which organizations are represented. Discuss the students' impressions of the stories. Did one issue dominate the week's news? Did journalists have different points of view on the same issue? Students will have learned to use print material as a resource tool, and will have discussed the role of journalists in reporting on issues.

• Fill a glass bottle (with a lid) with water and add a few drops of motor oil. Shake. Do the oil and water mix? Add a few drops of detergent and shake. Is the oil still there? Is it dispersed? Repeat using more oil. This activity should show that oil can be dispersed with detergents by breaking it up into tiny droplets and spreading it throughout the water. Is this a valid way of dealing with oil spills? Try other clean-up methods such as putting oil and water in a bowl and using a cotton swab to collect the oil or "corralling' the oil with string.

• Research how oil spills are actually cleaned up.

• Research some environmental effects of oil spills. Dip a feather in some oil. What happens to it? Would a feather covered in oil be able to insulate a bird?

• Discuss if we, as consumers, are in any way responsible for oil spills or other disasters such as tire fires. After this discussion read the class this quote from the Southam News Environment Project: "Close to 300 million litres of motor oil vanishes into the Canadian environment each year, much of it carelessly poured down sewers by do-it-yourself mechanics. That's almost eight times more oil than spilled when the Exxon Valdez ran aground off Alaska . . ."

Needs versus wants

To discuss the difference between items that we need and those that we want

Have students write definitions of "need" and "want". In small groups, discuss and compare the definitions.

In pairs, have one student choose a magazine ad for an item that is a "need" and the other choose an ad for an item that is a "want". The students write a comparison of the two ads. What did each ad emphasize in order to convince the reader to buy?

Students can design an ad for a product (either a "want" or a "need") for television or radio. They have to decide on the best words to describe their product — quick, fast, easy, disposable, durable, long-lasting. Ads can be performed to the class.

Make Earth Day every day

To generate ideas for celebrating Earth Day, and to plan such a celebration for the school or community

Earth Day began in the United States on April 22, 1970. More than 20 million Americans were mobilized to demand action on pollution and environmental quality. Since then, Earth Day has been celebrated on an annual basis all over the world. For example, in 1990 there was a conference on the disappearance of tropical rainforests in Costa Rica, schoolchildren in Mauritius planted trees, in Banff and Jasper, Alberta local groups held aerobics classes to raise money for projects to save forests both in Canada and abroad, and a team of climbers from the U.S., the Soviet Union, and China climbed Mt. Everest to collect garbage left from previous expeditions.

Brainstorm ways to celebrate Earth Day in your classroom, school, or community. Some ideas to consider: plant trees, start a recycling program, have car free days at the school, have garbage-free lunches, have a paper free day (use slates, do sidewalk art . . .), hold a career day on environment-related careers, have a recycle-a-thon or a bike-a-thon.

After the class has decided how it wishes to celebrate, students need to develop a plan to carry through the celebration: when will it be held? how long will it be? who will be invited? does somebody need to give permission? will there be a cost? how many volunteers are there? how will advertising be done?

Carrying out the project is not the final step. Incorporate some of the activities into the everyday operation of the school. Don't just save them for special celebrations!

Environmental activists

To research an environmental group and the activities in which it is involved

In small groups or individually, students choose a particular issue in which they are interested or a group about which they would like to know more. There are over 1800 different environmental groups in Canada. There are environmental networks in each province or students can look in the yellow pages for ideas.

Students should obtain information such as what are the group's activities? who belongs? what does it cost to join? what does the logo represent?

If possible, ask representatives of local groups to speak to the class.

A poster presentation of each environmental group chosen by the students would illustrate the activities of the groups.

Local Heroes

An optional but highly recommended beginning for this activity is to share either the book or the film, *The Man Who Planted Trees* by Jean Giono. Then you can discuss what individuals can do to help the environment. If there is an individual in the community who has made a personal commitment to the environment have the students interview the "local hero". What is this person doing? How did the project get started? Is it paid work? How much time does it take?

Managing our waste

Introduction

- More than 90% of packaging lands on the garbage pile within one year of its production.

- Recycling one tonne of paper saves 17 mature trees or 22t of wood.

- Using recycled scrap iron instead of iron ore to make new steel results in an 86% reduction in air pollution, a 76% reduction in water pollution and a 97% reduction in mining waste.

- $1.5 billion/year is spent on garbage disposal.

The garbage we create is very much a product of our consumer society and the onslaught of disposable items and excess packaging. Our landfills are rapidly reaching their capacity and the search for new sites is on. The increase in consumption and the production of huge amounts of garbage is largely a phenomenon of the developed world and Canadians are some of the "worst wasters" in the world. Canada produces about 27 million tonnes of garbage every year. Many products that we put in our landfills have used valuable resources and energy and most have created some form of pollution during their manufacture.

The amount of garbage we produce must be reduced. Luckily, this is one of the environmental problems where consumer "clout" really comes in to play. We can all reconsider our purchases and determine whether what we buy is placing as small an impact as possible on the environment.

Resource Sheet on Waste Management

MATERIAL	RESOURCES USED TO PRODUCE	OPTIONS FOR MANAGEMENT	BIODEGRADABLE?
Glass	sand, lime-stone, soda, ash	– dispose – reuse – recycle	no
Paper, cardboard	trees & chemicals	– dispose – reuse – recycle	yes
Aluminum cans	aluminum	– dispose – recycle	no
Steel cans ("tin")	iron & tin ores	– dispose – recycle	in 10-20 yrs.
Polystyrene foam	petro-chemicals & additives	– dispose	no
Hard plastic bottles & con-tainers	petro-chemicals	– dispose – some home reuse – recycle*	no
Organics	sun, water	– dispose – compost	yes
Plastic-coated cartons	trees, chemicals, petro-chemicals	– dispose	after a long period of time
Aerosol containers	steel & plastic	dispose	no

* Plastics are usually recycled only once and they are used in plastic "lumber", flower pots, outdoor furniture, fence posts, etc. Recycling plastics is problematic as there are so many types of plastic.

Source: B.C. Ministry of the Environment

ENERGY SAVED* BY RECYCLING	AIR POLLUTION* REDUCED BY RECYCLING	WATER POLLUTION* REDUCED BY RECYCLING
8%	20%	50%
23-70%	60-73%	15-61%
97%	96%	97%
47-75%	86%	75%
—	—	—
—	—	—
—	—	—
—	—	—
—	—	—

* Estimate of pollution reduction & energy savings by using recycled materials to produce new goods.

Waste words

Students will become familiar with words that are commonly used when discussing waste

Brainstorm with the students to make a list of all the synonyms for the word, waste (e.g. garbage, trash, scraps, debris, leftovers, junk, rubbish, litter, refuse, "misplaced resources"). Do some of the words sound better than others? Do they actually mean different things? Discuss the difference between waste and garbage.

Using a dictionary or thesaurus, students can research the definition of the following words. Also ask students to examine the prefixes and root words.

biodegradable (bio-degrade-able)
recycle (re-cycle)
renewable (re-new-able)
limited
sustainable

To ensure that the students have working definitions have them compose sentences for each word.

Write a definition of the word "away". Discuss with the students if there is such a thing as "away"? When something is thrown out is it really away? Who picks it up? Where does it go? How much does it cost? What would happen if it wasn't collected? What do they do with the garbage when it gets to its destination? Is it incinerated, recycled, buried, compacted? To better understand these concepts the students could draw individually the path of a piece of paper from the garbage can to the landfill site.

Weekly waste

To become aware of what we consume, what we waste, and what we can do to limit waste

Make arrangements with the school custodian to allow garbage to accumulate in the classroom for several days. Have six garbage cans in your class, one each for glass, paper, plastic, metal, food, and other. If your school does not support the idea of letting garbage accumulate, you could make this an ongoing project where garbage is analyzed and/or weighed at the end of every day. Place "garbage" into the appropriate cans.

Calculate by graphing and/or percentages, the quantities of each type of waste. This could be calculated by individual pieces, by volume or by mass. Estimate the amount of waste per week leaving your classroom and, by extension, your school. Estimate the amount per year.

Discuss the "3 Rs" with the class: reduce, reuse, and recycle. Think of some ways to reduce, reuse, or recycle some of the garbage in the class' pile.

What are some more "Rs"? (rethink, recover, reclaim, reject, recirculate, refuse, repair).

Make a collage or mural with some of the items that were thrown away and some alternatives for their disposal or use. If a hall bulletin board is available, present your findings to the rest of your school.

Find out the ultimate destination of this "garbage". What alternatives are available to throwing these items in the garbage? What would you do if there was no garbage collection?

The power of a package

To examine the purposes of packaging and the relationships among consumers, advertising, and packaging

For a day or two collect packaging separate from other garbage. How much of your garbage is packaging? (Packaging can contribute up to 50% by volume of our solid waste and it accounts for 10-15% of the price of a product.)

Brainstorm the purposes of packaging. Ideas could include: health requirements (sanitation), legal requirements, protection (prevent spoilage, contamination), communication/advertisement (identification), convenience, containment, theft prevention, distribution efficiency.

Collect some further example of packages and bring them in to class or use a catalogue, advertising flyer, or a visit to a local store to find examples of products which: use packaging for protection, need special packages for health reasons, have recyclable packaging, have excess packaging, have a "natural" package (i.e. fruit), have misleading packaging.

The class can combine its findings. Then students can choose one product that they feel uses inappropriate packaging, and design an alternative to this packaging. The new package should be evaluated. Are the materials recyclable, reusable, or biodegradable? Does the product actually need a package? Does the package still make the product attractive to the consumer? The class can write to the manufacturer telling the company about its new packaging idea.

Presto! Chango! Our resources become . . .

To examine the path of various items from raw product to finished product and the energy and materials used in its transportation and processing

Each student chooses a product that is used around the school or home, e.g. school construction materials, carpets, windows, paper, paint, picnic table, swing set, window glass. The item chosen should be traced back to the raw product and each stage in its transformation examined. For example, to make paper: cut trees — transport cut trees — chop up trees — make pulp — make paper — transport to store — drive to store — buy paper — use paper — dispose or recycle.

These are some of the questions students should answer:

What is the product made of?

Where do the raw materials come from?

Where is it made?

What sort of machines are used?

Does its manufacture cause pollution?

How was it transported to where it is being used?

What would we use if we didn't have this product?

Can we think of any improvements to the product?

What impact, if any, does the manufacturing process have on the environment?

What happens to the product if it is no longer used?

Students can illustrate their findings in comic strip style. Comic strips can then be cut up, block by block, and swapped with a friend to see if the correct sequence can be reconstructed to show the path from raw material to finished product.

Recycle a tree

Students will develop an understanding of the recycling process by recycling paper

Materials: pieces of nylon screening (plastic needlepoint canvas works well)

> *stapler*
> *blender, food processor, hand mixer, egg beater*
> *plastic tub or basin*
> *sponge*
> *iron*
> *newspaper or other types of paper (i.e. gift wrap, scrap paper, napkins, grocery bags, comics, crepe paper, envelopes, tissues, candy bar wrappers . . . experiment!)*
> *some vegetable peelings (potato, apple, carrot)*
> *towel*

Summarize some reasons we should recycle paper, such as (i) disposes of solid waste and reduces the amount going to landfills, (ii) conserves forest resources (for every tonne of paper recycled, 17 trees are saved), (iii) saves energy (one tonne of paper recycled saves enough energy to power an average home for 6 months), (iv) cuts down on air pollution.

1. Rip up paper into small bits. Half-fill the blender, or bowl if you are using a hand beater. Add the peelings of a potato, carrot, or apple; these will help to bind the paper. (You can also experiment by adding extra things like sparkles, pieces of ribbons, doilies, or confetti. If you use newspaper as the base, the finished paper will be quite grey; you might want to add food coloring or berry juice for color.)

2. Add enough water to cover the paper. Mix at a slow speed until you have a thick pulp. Add more water if your blender is working too hard.

3. Put about 10mm of water into the basin and lay the screen on the bottom. Dump the pulp on to the screen. Gently lift the screen and spread the pulp in a thin layer over the screen.

4. Cover a flat surface with newspaper and turn the screen over and dump the pulp (hopefully it's fairly flat and thin) onto the newspaper.
5. Try to mop up extra water with a sponge then leave the paper in a flat place to dry (it may take a few days). To speed up the process the paper can be ironed when it is almost dry.

The recycled paper can be used for artwork, cards, posters, or bookmarks.

The class can research the history of paper and paper making. A field trip can be organized to a paper recycling plant. A classroom visit can be made by an artist who makes paper.

EXTENSION

Have the class brainstorm a list of items that can be recycled, and what they can be recycled into. The following chart gives you some suggestions.

RESOURCE	RECYCLED INTO
paper	newsprint, paper, packaging, cardboard, shoeboxes, cereal boxes, home insulation, stiffeners in chocolate boxes and writing pads, boards for games like chess, some toilet paper and facial tissues, egg cartons
glass	glass
steel cans ("tin" cans)	steel
aluminum cans	aluminum
rubber	adhesives, asphalt, retread tires, sports surfaces
most food and garden wastes	compost (recycled soil and nutrients — a natural fertilizer)
some plastics	other plastics
oil	oil
food processing and farm wastes	animal feeds and fertilizers
textiles	new fabrics, flooring, roofing

Get growing

To learn about tree biology by building a human tree

The class builds a tree by acting out the various parts of the tree and working together to create a living, eating, breathing, and drinking tree. You act as the director to coordinate the activities of the various parts of the tree to see that they work together properly.

Heartwood: Choose two or three students to play the heartwood. The heartwood is the "mechanical support" of the tree — the inner core which provides the strength for the tree. These players stand with their backs to each other and act "strong" to fulfill their role of keeping the tree upright and tall.

Taproot: These primary roots grow as deep as possible into the ground and gather water for the tree from deep in the ground. They also work to anchor the tree. These players (3 or 4) sit at the base of the heartwood, facing outwards and also act strong. They make slurping noises to show that they are drinking water.

Lateral Roots: Lateral roots grow out from the tree and serve as support. Lateral roots also have tiny root hairs which seek water. Choose players with long hair. Have them lie on their backs with their feet up against the heartwood. Spread out their hair around their heads — this represents the root hairs. They should also make slurping noises.

Sapwood: Sapwood is also called xylem. The xylem draws water up from the roots and brings it up to the trees branches. Players stand in a circle around the heartwood, facing inwards, holding hands. After the roots "slurp" up the water, the sapwood brings it up the tree. Holding hands, they crouch down, then stand up and raise their arms, saying "sluuuuuuurp".

Cambium: The cambium layer is the part of the tree which is growing. Each year the tree adds a new layer to the sapwood and the phloem and the tree grows outward from the centre. Players stand in a circle with their backs to the sapwood. They move their arms outwards to represent the growth of the tree.

Phloem: The phloem is the part of the tree that carries food made in the leaves (via photosynthesis) and distributes it to the rest of the tree. Players stand in a circle facing inwards, around the cambium. They hold their hands over their heads and shake them — these are the leaves making food. They take the food down by bringing their arms quickly down by their sides and bending at the knees to bring their body and arms down to the ground. They can make a "whump" sound at the same time.

Bark: The bark is the outer layer which protects the tree. Have the players stand in a circle around the rest of the tree, facing outwards. They should have their elbows out and act as if they are "protecting" the tree.

Getting the tree working: The director should go through, in order, all parts of the tree. The director will shout out the actions and the tree begins working.

Discuss some of the things from which the bark might have to protect the tree (insects, disease, fire, etc.). You may want to introduce some insects who try to break through the bark, only to be turned away (hopefully) by the bark.

Logo lingo

To study the use of logos, specifically using the example of the universal logo for recycling:

The recycling logo is a stylized moebius strip. The moebius strip, which demonstrates an infinite or endless surface, is named after August Ferdinand Moebius, a German mathematician who discovered the one-sided strip in 1858. The strip is made by giving a strip of paper a half twist and joining the ends. The moebius loop is used as the recycling logo as it symbolizes the endless use and re-use of materials as being the ultimate goal of recycling. The three arrows represent the three kinds of recyclable substances: gases, liquids, and solids.

Brainstorm reasons why organizations use logos. Have a selection of logos available for study. Study the logo for recycling. Interpret why this logo has been chosen to symbolize recycling.

Make a moebius strip:

- Give each student a strip of paper about 30cm long and 2-3cm wide. Make a loop by taping the ends together.

- Cut the loop in half around the middle. No one is probably surprised when you get two loops.
- Using a second strip, make a half-twist in the paper before you tape the loop together. Now cut this loop down the centre. What happens?

Starting a recycling program

To learn the process of setting up a small scale recycling program in the school

Brainstorm the positive and negative aspects of recycling. Some ideas that might be generated are given.

POSITIVE

— conserves natural resources
— saves energy
— protects the environment
— can generate money
— creates jobs
— disposes of solid waste that would normally go to the landfill

NEGATIVE

— may cost more money than it generates
— more organizational time
— takes up space for storage

Discuss how the class should go about setting up a paper recycling program. What would be the logical sequence?
- Find a market that will take the paper. Look in the yellow pages. What will they take? (newsprint, office paper, cardboard?) How much do they pay? How should it be delivered to them? In what quantity?
- What would the class do with the money generated?
- Once your program is operating consider adding other items like glass, tin, aluminum or beverage containers.

Getting rid of waste

To examine three methods for waste disposal: landfilling, incineration, and recycling/composting

Discuss the methods for getting rid of solid waste and the advantages and disadvantages of the methods. The students may generate some of the following ideas:

LANDFILLING — *Advantages:*
— low cost
— can be reclaimed to some extent
— fairly low maintenance
— most type of wastes can be put in landfills

Disadvantages:
— requires a lot of land and there is a shortage of land available for landfills
— leachates may flow off landfill into water bodies
— decomposition can create methane gas which can be explosive
— no one wants them nearby
— waste of resources (items that could be recovered and reused)

INCINERATION — *Advantages:*
— reduces the amount of waste, therefore the requirement for landfill space can be reduced
— the heat generated can be recovered

Disadvantages:
— air pollution (ash and gases)
— can only process items that will burn
— little control over what is being burned so some materials *may* be producing harmful gases
— waste of resources (items that could be recycled/recovered)
— higher cost

RECYCLING — *Advantages:*
— conserves natural resources
— saves energy
— less impact on the environment
— can generate money
— creates jobs

Disadvantages:
— labor intensive
— more organizational time

Investigate how waste is disposed of in your community. Who collects the garbage? Where does it go? Who pays for the collection? How much does it cost? How much is disposed of daily? Are there any materials being recycled?

Make a mini-landfill in the classroom:

— Put some soil in each of four drinking glasses.

— Bury household waste in the soil so that you can see it against the glass. Make sure there is soil above and below. You could use 1 cm of wastes such as plaster, food scraps, paper, glass, aluminum.

— Add some water to dampen the "landfill".

— Cover the containers with foil or plastic wrap.

— Predict what will happen to each of the items.

— Observe the items daily.

— Were the predictions accurate?

Set up and operate a compost pile. Ask students to use library resources for ideas on how to do it.

Arrange a tour of your local waste disposal or treatment site; or visit a recycling depot if one exists.

Have the students imagine that they could develop the waste management strategy for their community. How would they do it?

Musical recycling

To create musical instruments from items that would normally be thrown out

Students can create instruments and use them in a class band. They can write a song about recycling.

BELLS AND CHIMES

Hang pieces of metal (forks, knives, horseshoes, scrap) from a wire and hit with a spoon.

CANASTA

Attach two big buttons on either end of a strip of cardboard. Fold the cardboard in half. Click the buttons together.

RATTLES

Put dried corn in an empty plastic lemon or lime juice bottle. Decorate.

Staple two paper or aluminum pie plates together with beans inside. Attach to a stick. Decorate.

Papier mâché an old lightbulb. When dry, decorate. Bang the bulb on a hard surface until the glass breaks.

Yoghurt or cottage cheese containers can be filled with beans.

Nail bottle caps in 2s and 3s loosely to a square stick or broom handle.

CYMBALS

Bang old pot lids together. Decorate them with ribbons and streamers.

MARACAS

Use tubes from toilet rolls. Cover one end with aluminum foil and fill the tube with beans, peas, or rice. Cover the other end, decorate and shake!

POP BOTTLE WHISTLE

Blow across the mouth of a pop bottle.

MOUTH ORGANS/KAZOOS

Fold wax paper or airmail paper over a comb. Put it up to your lips and hum.

Make a kazoo from a cardboard tube. Decorate the tube. Put a piece of wax paper over one end, secured with an elastic band. Hum a tune through the other end.

TAMBOURINE

Glue two paper plates together. Punch holes around the rim and attach bells or bottle caps with wire, ribbon, or string. Paint the plates.

DRUMS

Use a plastic milk jug. Beat with a wooden spoon.

RHYTHM STICKS

Use scrap pieces of wood or dowelling. Paint or decorate. Hit together.

Cover wooden blocks with pieces of sandpaper. Attach using nails or glue. Rub together for sound.

XYLOPHONE

Fill jars full of water to varying levels. Use colored water for fun. Strike with a pencil, spoon, or stick.

SPOONS

Nest two spoons inside one another.

BUGLE

Join a piece of old garden hose to a plastic or metal funnel with duct tape.

GUITAR

Use an empty tissue box as a guitar. Stretch some rubber bands (of different sizes) lengthwise across the opening of the box. The lighter the bands, the better the sound.

Fast-food garbage

To look at our society's need for items that are fast and convenient, and the problems this can create with package pollution

Discuss why our society has fast-food outlets, convenience foods, convenience stores, and disposable items.

Divide the class into groups. Visit a number of fast-food restaurants. Order some food, bring it back to class. How much food is there? How much packaging? Weigh both. Take pictures of the food and the packaging. Are there some alternatives to all this packaging? Let the restaurant managers know the findings of the class by writing a letter.

Supermarket savvy

To examine prepared and convenience foods and the energy that has gone in to their production and packaging

Have students look at the convenience foods that one household might buy on one day. Separate the actual food from the packaging. Take or draw pictures of both piles. Weigh the piles. What are some suggestions for reducing the packaging?

Look at food advertising. What do advertisers emphasize to make us buy their product? Do they use gimmicks, such as fancy containers or prizes?

Compare the cost of raw potatoes, frozen french fries, potato chips, and french fries from a fast food store. What are the reasons for the price difference?

Discuss some of the monetary, social, and environmental consequences of convenience foods.

The n.i.m.b.y. syndrome

To examine the social consequences of and public opposition to sanitary landfill sites near residential areas.

Many landfill sites are rapidly filling to capacity. Consequently, new landfill sites are needed. Many people have what has been called "the N.I.M.B.Y. syndrome" — Not In My Backyard. These people do not want landfill sites anywhere near their homes and community.

Discuss why people would not want landfill sites near their homes. What are some potential problems of landfill construction and operation? Some ideas: traffic, noise, dust, aesthetic loss, declining property values, groundwater contamination, hazardous waste pollution. (These fears have all been justified over time but modern landfill design, construction, and management minimize most problems.)What are some alternatives to having landfills? Would alternatives cost more?

Ask the students to write a paragraph on how to solve the landfill question from the perspective of the following people:
— a politician
— a concerned resident
— the president of the local environmental group
— the town's waste management director
— a Grade 6 student who is concerned about the growing amount of garbage in our society.

Household waste

To examine the amount of waste thrown out in the home, and to devise ways to reduce the amount

Discuss the average amount of garbage that is thrown away by each person each day (approx. 2.5 kg/day). What is thrown away? Use the following garbage breakdown "wheel" as a reference. Discuss what makes something trash.

It's All Going In The Garbage: What We Throw Away

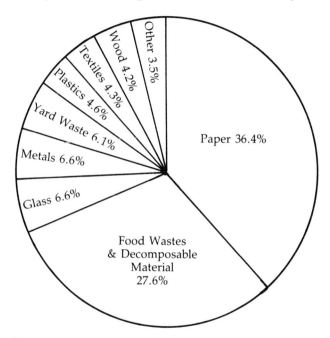

Source: Environment Council of Alberta

Research how much households pay for garbage collection. What would happen if households were charged per bag of garbage?

Devise an easy-to-use chart so that students can list what goes into their household garbage can. Have each student create a plan to reduce the amount of garbage that leaves the house. They should consider reducing and rejecting items purchased, recycling, reusing and composting. Students should evaluate their families' plans. Did their families cooperate? Was their garbage reduced?

The toxics tour

To examine the hazardous and special wastes that are all around us, and that we often use in our daily lives

Industries are often blamed for the plethora of chemicals entering our environment, but collectively households are equal contributors. The average Canadian household has up to 45 aerosols and another 24 non-aerosol cleansers, solvents, and other household products.

Most of these products have components which are harmful to human or environmental health.

Advertising has greatly influenced the amount of these products we have in our homes. We are led to believe we need them all to keep our bodies and homes free of germs and "squeaky clean". Like industrial chemicals, household chemicals end up in our sewer systems or garbage dumps and do their part in upsetting sensitive ecosystems.

Many of these products are just not necessary or have safe, non-toxic, and inexpensive alternatives. Just ask our grandparents what they used!

Good resources for this activity include:

The Household Hazardous Waste Wheel: lists common household chemicals, the hazardous ingredients, alternatives, and disposal options; it is available at $5.00 U.S. from
Environmental Hazards Management Institute,
10 Newmarket Road,
P.O. Box 932,
Durham, New Hampshire
03824
(603) 868-1496

Save-It: Household Hazardous Wastes and Alternatives to Household Chemicals is available free of charge from
Environment Canada,
Communications Department,
Twin Atria #2,
2nd Floor, 4999-98 Avenue,
Edmonton, Alberta
T6B 2X3
(403) 468-8075

Local environmental groups often have suggestions for environmentally-friendly cleaning products.

Review what these symbols mean with the students.

 TOXIC OR POISONOUS
poisonous or lethal to animals, plants, and humans

 FLAMMABLE
liquids that can ignite

 REACTIVE OR EXPLOSIVE
can create an explosion or release deadly vapours when mixed

 CORROSIVE
eat away at other materials

The symbols for hazardous products have been shown within the "danger" outline shape. These symbols may also be shown within a "warning" and a "caution" outline shape.

Warning   Caution

Have students make a list of products in their homes that may be hazardous wastes. Divide the house into different rooms: garage/basement, kitchen, bathroom, and laundry room. Things to consider: motor oil, antifreeze, old batteries, paint, insecticides, herbicides, drain cleaners, aerosols, household disinfectants, window cleaners, oven cleaners, tub and tile cleaners, turpentine, moth balls, lighter fluid. Do they have any of the above symbols on them?

Have students research the proper method of disposal. Should these chemicals go down the drain? Is there a hazardous waste disposal station in your community?

Each student can choose one of the products from the class list of household products. Each should research what it is made of, the proper disposal method, why it is potentially hazardous, and if there are any alternatives. The class can compile a booklet for distribution to friends and family on environmentally-friendly household products, based on its research.

Discovering the link between habitats and wildlife

Introduction

- The world's deserts are growing at a rate of six million hectares each year
- Fourteen hectares of forest are cut down worldwide every minute
- Twenty-four billion tonnes of productive topsoil are lost worldwide every year
- At least one species is lost forever every hour of every day; some estimates say as many as 45 species of plants and animals will die each day
- It is estimated that the earth supports between 5 and 80 million species; of these scientists have found and named only 1.5 million
- Tropical rainforests cover about 7% of the earth's surface but between 50 and 80% of the planet's species inhabit these forests. Our land is under constant stress from the pressures placed on it by humans. As of 1990, there were about 5 billion people living on the earth. People move into areas where animals and plants live, or used to live. To make way for people and our "needs" as consumers, forests are cut down, wetlands are drained, and more and more land is paved over. All these activities are adversely affecting our environment.

Species are disappearing at an astronomical rate and more and more habitats are lost. The World Wildlife Fund estimates that 7 of every 10 species that become extinct do so because of loss of habitat.

Loss of temperate and tropical rainforests can result in soil depletion, erosion, loss of species, and a disruption in the earth's water cycles. As well, since trees "breathe" carbon dioxide, their loss means an increase of carbon dioxide in the atmosphere which contributes to the problem of global warming.

As forests disappear, soil erosion accelerates. Valuable topsoil blows away, soil becomes compacted and less able to grow crops. As a result it becomes more difficult to feed the huge numbers of people on the planet. Loss of agricultural land is also felt in Canada. In Canada only 9% of the land mass is arable but nearly 19% of this was converted to uses other than agriculture between 1961 and 1981.

Parks and nature preserves set aside small pieces of land for future generations but is this all that we want to leave as a legacy for our children? People enjoy visiting such natural areas which is shown by the many people visiting parks across the country each year. We should, however, not just consider parks as land worth saving; we should look at all land as a valuable resource that is worth our concern.

A home for wildlife

To examine different habitats for wildlife and plants; students will realize that many animals and plants become endangered because of loss of habitat

A habitat is the arrangement of food, water, shelter or cover, and space (territory). These are the basic needs for wildlife and all animals have specific requirements. Many things affect wildlife populations, including overhunting, introduction of new non-native species which compete with native wildlife, pollution, and the destruction of wildlife habitats.

Habitats are vital parts of ecosystems. It is difficult for animals to adapt to changed habitats as quickly as the old habitats are being destroyed. Habitats are adversely affected by a number of factors including: pressures of an increasing population, poverty, greed, and short-sighted political actions. Examples of habitat destruction include: deforestation, draining wetlands and lakes, flooding watersheds, and pollution.

Discuss the concept of habitat with the class. What is the habitat for humans? List what we *need* to survive.

Students should choose an animal that interests them. Play animal charades with the class and try to identify the animals being acted out. Try the activity in pairs and share the role playing of the animal.

They should research their animal to discover the following:
— food and water requirements
— cover/shelter (sleeping, nesting, feeding)
— space (territory)
— predators (their "enemies")
— human activities that disturb them
— disease and parasites
— is the animal endangered?

Students can create a poster presentation, diorama, or habitat booklet describing their animal's habitat requirements. They can create a map or drawing of what the habitat looks like.

The class can discuss some ways to slow or stop the destruction of wildlife habitat, and what the class can do.

A personal place in nature

To observe a natural area over time and monitor the changes that it goes through

Students choose a natural area near their home or school. They will visit and monitor the area over a period of time (a year would be desirable, but not necessary). Students may benefit from using a magnifying glass. They should keep a field notebook of:
— plants (large and small)
— animals (signs of them as well as actual sightings; don't forget the insects!)
— weather
— available water
— the smells, sounds, and view of each area
— the rocks; soil type

The field notebooks can include drawings, poetry, anything that relates to the particular nature space.

Students monitor the changes through the seasons and "improve" their areas by keeping them clean of litter.

Nature spaces

To research why nature preserves and parks are established, how they are run, and who uses them

Students choose a local, provincial, or national park or nature preserve to investigate why it was established. Was it set up to protect wildlife? plants? habitat? special natural features? Who maintains the park? Who uses the park? How is the park used? Who owns the land?

Students in groups can develop a plan to create a park or nature preserve in an area that is special to them. How would they run it? Would they allow people to visit or would they put the land aside for protection? Why do they think the area should be preserved?

If possible arrange a visit to a local park or nature preserve.

Micro-environments

To study nature from a bug's eye view

Students can make a bug catcher. A small square is cut from an old pair of panty hose, and placed over the end of a 8mm length of a small-sized straw. Fit a larger straw over this end and secure with scotch tape.

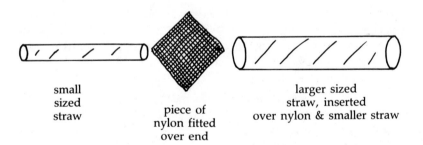

small sized straw

piece of nylon fitted over end

larger sized straw, inserted over nylon & smaller straw

To catch bugs, place the large end of the bug catcher over the bug and suck up on the smaller straw. The bug will get caught against the nylon — not down your throat. Put your finger over the end of the straw to capture the bug and gently place it in a bug box or plastic container.

Students can make picture frames from construction paper.

Choose a spot in the school yard or a nearby park where students can place their frames on the ground — this will be their micro-environment. Students study any bugs captured in their micro-environment. They can draw pictures of the bugs and identify them if possible. The bugs are released after being studied. Students describe the plants, rocks, animal signs, etc. that they saw in their micro-environment.

What good are insects? What would our world look like if there weren't any insects? Students can research to find out.

Students can write a story describing the micro-environment from the point of view of a bug. What would a piece of dirt or a blade of grass look like to a bug?

Making room for wildlife

To create a wildlife habitat
Review the components of habitats ("A home for wildlife" is a good activity to review).

With the blessing of your school and some help from volunteers, a wildlife habitat can be created in your schoolyard. (This could also be done as a project for students at home).

Some ideas:
— plant flowers, trees and shrubs for shelter and food (i.e. butterflies like brightly colored flowers and hummingbirds are attracted to red plants)
— keep a brush pile of twigs, leaves, and branches for small animals to use as cover
— add bird baths and bird houses
— rock piles can attract snakes, amphibians, and reptiles
— add a pond complete with aquatic plants
— cover chain link fences by planting flowering vines

Take a before and after picture of your wildlife habitat. Monitor the wildlife that visits.

Soil erosion

To demonstrate the importance of trees and plants in preventing soil erosion

Fill two wooden boxes or pie plates or large baking pans with soil. Plant grass seed in one box and water every other day. When the seed has sprouted (about 3 weeks) set the boxes up on a slight angle. Place buckets at the base of the boxes. Pour equal amounts of water on the surface of each box. Catch the runoff with the buckets. Examine which container contains the most soil. Which contains the most water? How has the grass kept the soil and water in the box?

Discuss what activities might cause soil erosion (e.g. deforestation, construction, strip mining).

Research some ways to prevent soil erosion due to wind and water.

Celebrate Arbor Day

To introduce students to Arbor Day, its history and purpose, and to study the aesthetic and environmental values of trees

Arbor Day was introduced by J. Sterling Morton in Nebraska in 1872. Morton wanted to plant trees in his state as he recognized that trees would benefit the farmers by providing windbreaks and by preventing soil erosion. People would also enjoy trees for their shade and beauty.

On a monument in Morton's memory is the following inscription: "Other holidays repose upon the past. Arbor Day proposes for the future." Since Arbor Day began, millions of trees have been planted to recognize the value of trees and the importance of conservation. Many areas in both Canada and the U.S. celebrate Arbor Day in April or May. The legal holiday in Nebraska is on April 22, Morton's birthday.

Discuss the background of Arbor Day. Mention that "arbor" is Latin for tree. Discuss the meaning of the inscription on Morton's monument.

In groups have the students brainstorm positive things about trees, such as aesthetics, absorb carbon dioxide, release oxygen, hold soil, water quality, temperature regulation, prevent erosion, protect wildlife, habitat for wildlife.

Read the book, *The Giving Tree* by Shel Silverstein. Although it is an easy read, the message is ageless. Have children perform the story as a reader's theatre or a play or have them storytell and present it to younger students in the school.

Celebrate Arbor Day. As a group decide on a special way to celebrate. Local/provincial forestry associations and tree nurseries often have trees available for school groups to plant. Ideas include single tree plantings, group tree plantings, clean-ups, parades, hikes or other special events.

If you do plant a tree keep a notebook and monitor its progress. Include: height, breadth, when the first buds appear in the spring, when the leaves fall off, what insects, birds or other animals appear on the tree, the texture, color, and any injuries on the bark, whether other plants grow on or under the tree. If you don't plant a tree students could adopt a tree near their school or home and monitor it. A leaf rubbing and bark rubbing could be done for the notebook.

Make trees to celebrate Arbor Day. Place a drop of ink on a piece of paper. Blow on the ink with a straw to make a pattern like a tree trunk and some branches. Allow the tree to dry for several minutes. Mix up some tempera paints in "leaf" colors; dab "leaves" on with a brush or sponge.

Discuss if a tree has any value when it is dead. This is an opportune time to discuss death, decay, and recycling in nature. Standing dead trees are invaluable for woodpeckers (the bugs in dying trees are an excellent food source) and cavity-dwelling animals and birds. Fallen dead trees are recycled back into the nutrient base of forests through the process of decay. If possible, go on a field trip and examine a fallen tree. Record how many different types of plants, insects, and other creatures you find living on this tree.

Read *The Man Who Planted Trees* by Jean Giono. This is a wonderful story of a man who took it upon himself to replant what was once a forest near his home. How did students react to the story? What did they think compelled this man to plant all these trees?

How it used to be

To research the history of the school yard

Investigate what the school yard used to look like before it was developed to its current use. Were there other buildings on the site? Was there forest?

Interview older residents who can tell the class the history of the area. Collect pictures and visit a local museum or archives.

Students can create a story of the school yard history using storyboarding. The story can be written from the point of view of a person, an animal, a bird, a rock on the site, an insect in the soil — anything! Did the students think the site has been improved? Why or why not?

Going, going, gone?

To research endangered or threatened species, and why they are in trouble

Discuss what might cause species to become endangered or extinct. Some ideas: loss of habitat (encroachment of cities, deforestation, strip mining, draining of wetlands), overhunting, competition from non-native species (introduction of exotic species), and pollution.

Students can research some species that are extinct in Canada. They include: Dawson caribou, sea mink, passenger pigeon, great auk, labrador duck, *Atlantic gray whale, *Atlantic walrus, *black-footed ferret and *swift fox. Why did they become extinct in Canada?

Students can choose a species that is endangered or threatened in Canada and find out as much as they can about its habitat and why it is in trouble. Some endangered Canadian species: bowhead whale, eastern cougar, St. Lawrence River beluga whale, wood bison, Vancouver Island marmot, Eskimo curlew, mountain plover, spotted owl, whooping crane, cucumber tree, heart-leaved plantain, small white lady's slipper. Some threatened Canadian species: maritime woodland caribou, peary caribou, Newfoundland pine marten, prairie long-tailed weasel,

*These species are considered extirpated in Canada. This means they do not exist in their original habitat in Canada but do exist elsewhere.

burrowing owl, ferruginous hawk, roseate tern, red mulberry, sweet pepperbush.

A good source for further information is the World Wildlife Fund, 60 St. Clair Ave. E. Suite 201, Toronto, Ontario, M4T 1N5.

Dioramas, models, paintings, collages, or posters can be created about the chosen species, what its habitat is, and why it is in trouble. If possible, sounds can be included.

Students devise a plan to protect their species. What needs to happen for it to survive? Why should we care whether the species survives or not? Would a media campaign to advertise the fate of the species be helpful to its survival? If so, devise an appropriate media campaign.

Ask students to imagine a time in which there are no trees left and the air and water is polluted. They can design a bird or animal that would be capable of living in such an environment.

Trees in the developing world

To look at the importance of trees to people in the developing world
In many countries forests form the basis for their civilization. Indeed, we need only to look at the many aboriginal groups of Canada to see how dependent on the forests their culture is. From forests, people in developing countries get fuel, materials for construction, fruit, nuts, vegetables, fodder for their animals, oil, resins, gums, rubber, rattan, bamboo . . . the list goes on. As well, the forests regulate watersheds, water supplies, agricultural lands and soil.

Why then do we hear so much about droughts or clear-cut logging in developing countries? The answer is a complex one, and not one that can be given justice in the scope of this book. It is, however, a question that should be asked. Forests and, in particular, rainforests truly are the "lungs of the earth" and their plight needs to be addressed.

Some reasons for deforestation in developing countries: clearance for cattle ranching, clearance for crops, commercial timber logging, land speculation, large scale construction projects, growing demands by population on forests.

In many developing countries it is the women who have to travel to the forests to get firewood. In the state of Uttar Pradesh in India in 1974 women learned that a stand of forest was going to be cut to make way for a commercial development. The women, fully realizing what this would mean for their survival, went into the forests, joined hands and hugged the trees. The women told the contractors that if they wanted the trees they must take them too. This is called the Chipko ("to hug") movement. The contractors turned away and the forest was saved.

Brainstorm a list of things that people in some developing countries receive from forests.

Discuss how the loss of a forest would affect people who depended on it. Discuss the Chipko movement in India. Would the students be willing to do what those women did to save a forest? Are there any other people who are willing to give their lives for the environment?

Research tropical rainforests. Save newspaper and magazine clippings Why are people so concerned about the clearing of tropical rainforests? Some ideas:

— tropical rainforests regulate water cycles: they retain moisture and slowly release it
— without the trees, there is nothing to hold the soil
— many species (yet undiscovered) live in the tropical rainforests (the biological diversity is incredibly high in rainforests; in one hectare there may be as many as 300 species of trees and thousands of species of animals, insects and plants); it is estimated that 1—24 species become extinct every day.
— many of our medicines have been based on tropical plants
— rainforests are home to many people
— the burning of trees contributes to global warming
— the loss of such large areas of trees contributes to global warming

Learning more about acid rain

Introduction

- There are at least 14 000 biologically dead acidified lakes in Canada.

- Acid rain falls on 55% of eastern Canada's forests and they are showing substantial damage.

- Acid rain has cost as much as $7 billion a year in architectural damage in the eastern United States

- 84% of the most productive farmland in eastern Canada receives high levels of acid rain; Environment Canada estimates damage at $1 billion each year.

- More than 80% of Quebec's sugar bush has been affected by acid rain.

Most Canadians have heard of acid rain, but do we really know what it is, or how it is caused? As the name describes, it is rain, or more accurately precipitation, that has become acidic. This "rain" is severely damaging lakes, forests, wildlife, plants, buildings and monuments, and can aggravate respiratory ailments and other health concerns in humans.

When fossil fuels (coal, oil, and natural gas) are burned, sulphur dioxide (SO_2) and nitrogen oxide (NO_x) are released. In the atmosphere they mix with water vapor, sunlight, oxygen and other gases, and create sulphuric acid and nitric acid which return to the earth as acid precipitation.

The most common sources of sulphur dioxide emissions are

ore smelters and coal-burning power stations. Oxides of nitrogen originate from residential and commercial heating (fuel combustion for heating purposes), vehicle exhaust, and power plants.

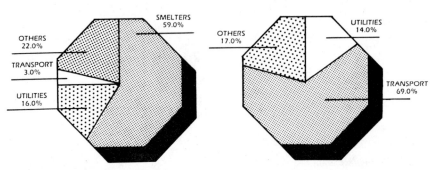

1980 EASTERN CANADIAN SO₂ EMISSIONS BY SOURCE

SMELTERS 59.0%
OTHERS 22.0%
TRANSPORT 3.0%
UTILITIES 16.0%

1980 EASTERN CANADIAN NOₓ EMISSIONS BY SOURCE

UTILITIES 14.0%
OTHERS 17.0%
TRANSPORT 69.0%

Acid precipitation doesn't recognize boundaries. Because of the action of winds and weather systems, acid precipitation often does not fall where it is produced. In Canada it is estimated that more than half of the acid deposition in eastern Canada originates in the U.S. But, Canadians are big contributors too; 10—25% of the acid rain in parts of the U.S. originates in Canada. Researchers have also found acid pollution in arctic regions which are hundreds of kilometres from any factories or cities.

In North America and Europe, acid rain has "killed" lakes by making them so acidic that no plants or fish can live in them. The environmental group, Friends of the Earth, states that there are at least 14 000 biologically dead lakes in Canada. About 5000 more are damaged and 350 000 are considered vulnerable. Many of the lakes more seriously affected are located in Ontario, Quebec, and Nova Scotia.

When acid precipitation falls on the soil, it increases the acidity of the soil making it easier for nutrients to be leached out. Damage occurs in soil, and also when the rain hits the leaves, needles, and bark of trees.

One of the more important plants that is being affected by acid rain is the sugar maple. Our flag sports a maple leaf, and maple syrup and other maple products are an important industry in eastern Canada and the United States. Approximately 80% of the sugar bush in Quebec and 60% in New Brunswick has been affected by acid rain. Acid precipitation also damages forests and croplands. Environment Canada estimates that 84% of the most productive agricultural lands in eastern Canada receive higher than acceptable levels of acid precipitation.

Acid shock to lakes and soils is also a serious problem. When snow accumulates during the winter so does the acid trapped within. When the snow melts the acid is released into soil and water and creates an environment many more times acidic than weeks before. This can kill insects, frogs, fish, and other creatures.

Acid precipitation has also been blamed for damage to many buildings. The precipitation corrodes and deteriorates building materials including cement, plastic, brick, stone, and metal. In Europe, damage to buildings and other items such as metal bells (which put the bells out of tune) is a particularly serious problem. Damage to buildings is also becoming a problem in eastern Canada. A House of Commons sub-committee studying acid rain estimated that damage to building materials due to acid rain was $285 million annually.

Canadian and American officials are introducing measures to control acid rain emissions. In March 1985, Prime Minister Mulroney stated that Canada would introduce a program to cut acid rain emissions in half by 1994. In June 1989, President Bush proposed that the United States would work to reduce emissions by half by the year 2000. Final legislation on acid rain control measures, including a U.S./Canada bilateral acid rain accord are being worked out.

We all contribute to the acid rain problem. We drive cars, we buy the products produced by large factories and smelters, and we heat our homes. It is estimated that more than fifty million tonnes of sulphur and nitrogen oxides are produced annually in North America.

Recycling, saving electricity, and reducing the use of our cars (basically using less energy and using it more efficiently) can help to reduce acid rain. The average household can lessen its contribution to the acid rain problem by five tonnes just by recycling its cans, bottles, and paper. Making new products from old takes a lot less energy and fewer resources.

The acid test

To introduce the concepts of acids and bases and to test various compounds to deduce whether they are an acid or a base, and introduce the concept of pH

"Clean" rain usually has a pH of 5.6. It is slightly acidic because of the presence of dissolved carbon dioxide, which is naturally present in the atmosphere. The pH scale describes acidity and is based on the concentration of hydrogen (H+) ions in a solution. The scale runs from 0-14 and the midpoint (7) is neutral. The scale is logarithmic, so small numerical changes indicate large changes in acidity. For example, pH 4 is 10 times more acidic than pH 5 and 100 times more acidic than pH 6. The average pH of rainfall in Canada is between 4 and 4.5; in much of southern Ontario the average annual acidity is 4.2.

In some areas nature can cope with acid rain. In areas where lakes and soil are slightly alkaline (usually in areas high in limestone) the acid precipitation will be neutralized in the soil and water. Many areas, however, do not have the natural capability to deal with large influxes of acid precipitation and environmental effects will result.

Aquatic systems are affected if the pH drops below 6. Few fish can reproduce below pH 5. Below pH 4.5 most aquatic life will die.

Discuss the concepts of acid and base. Acids familiar to the class might include vinegar and lemon juice. Bases might include baking soda.

Divide the class into pairs and have them prepare and test various compounds with litmus paper to see whether they are acids or bases. If no litmus paper is available, you can make an acid/base indicator from red cabbage; the recipe is given at the end of the activity.

Some compounds that can be used are aspirin, soft drinks, egg whites, sugar, distilled water, juices, lemonade, baking soda, vinegar, toothpaste, salt, tea, coffee, milk.

Prepare the substances as follows: liquids — use as is; powders — dissolve 5 ml in 150 ml of water; tablets — crush and add to 150 ml of water. Put substances in baby food jars and label. Acids turn blue litmus paper red. Bases turn red litmus paper blue. Substances which are neutral do not change the color of the litmus paper. Record the findings on an activity sheet.

Discuss the pH scale as a way to measure acids and bases. In the same groups and using the same substances, have students measure the pH using pH paper. Record the results on an activity sheet. Have the students add pure battery acid to their scale at pH 1 and ammonia at pH 11.

Have a student test the pH of the rainwater from your area. Is it acidic? Is it more acidic than pH 5.6? Discuss whether you have acid rain in your community or not.

Have students add to their activity sheets the pH levels at which the following creatures can no longer live or are severely dehabilitated:

opposum shrimp pH 5.8
crayfish pH 5.7
amphipods pH 5.6
bullfrog pH 4.1
spotted salamander pH 4.1
fish pH 5.0

Discuss what the loss of some or all of the above creatures would mean for a food chain. What would fish-eating birds or mammals eat? What would fish eat?

If you live in an area where acid precipitation is not a problem try finding a school in an area where it is. Team up with the school as "Acid Precipitation Pen Pals". Collect rain or snow samples, test them for pH and swap results. Keep in contact with the class and monitor pH changes throughout the year, especially if their community is trying to reduce acid precipitation.

Homemade Acid/Base Indicator

Red cabbage juice is a good substance to use as an acid/base indicator. The chemical reaction between cabbage juice and what you add to it will cause the juice to change color. Acids turn the indicator red and bases turn the indicator green/blue.

1. Put 5 or 6 red cabbage leaves and 500 mL of water in a pot, cover and bring to a boil. Let simmer for 15 minutes.
2. Let the mixture cool, then squeeze any remaining juice in the leaves into the water. Store the juice in a container and refrigerate if you won't be using it immediately.
3. Cut strips from a paper towel and soak them with cabbage juice. Let them dry. Once dry use strips just like litmus paper.

What goes up must come down

To explain and simulate the water cycle and why air pollution returns to us as acid precipitation

Discuss the water cycle using the following diagram.

To help students visualize the water cycle begin heating water in a kettle. Put cold water and/or ice cubes in a saucepan. When the water is boiling, hold the saucepan just above the steam. (Keep your hands away from the steam.) Water droplets will form on the bottom of the saucepan and soon there will be "rain".

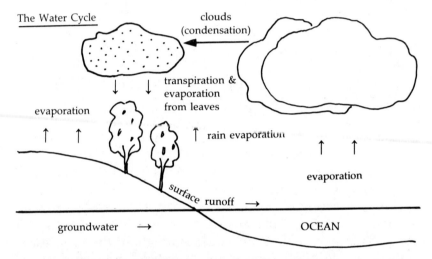

Have the students draw the water cycle you have just demonstrated and compare it to the natural water cycle.

Brainstorm the different forms of precipitation (e.g. fog, dew, rain, snow, sleet, hail). Explain that acid deposition is not just in the form of rain, but in all forms of precipitation.

Explaining fossil fuels

To understand what fossil fuels are, how they are created, how we use them, and how they contribute to acid precipitation

Coal, oil, and natural gas are all fossil fuels — they were formed from what once were plants and animals. Millions of years ago plants and animals grew in swamps and warm, shallow seas. As they died, many were covered by sediment and did not decompose in the same manner that organisms dying in the presence of oxygen would decompose. Over many millions of years (through the effects of time and pressure) these plants and animals have been changed into coal (plants), oil and natural gas (animals) — what we now remove from the ground and burn as fossil fuels to heat our homes, fuel our cars, buses, planes, and to make plastic.

Sulfur and nitrogen, as well as other elements, are released into the air as gases when fossil fuels are burned and this contributes to acid deposition.

Using coal as an example discuss the process of the formation of a fossil fuel. Perform ''The Coal-Making Song'' to reinforce the process of coal formation.

THE COAL-MAKING SONG
© 1985 by Monica Field

Once u-pon a time when the world was young, The
ma-king of coal ——— was just be-gun,— The
din — o - saurs and the swamp-y trees were
hap-py in the sun and the warm, south— breeze.———
Rum-ble, rum-ble, rum—— ble,———
Rum-ble, rum-ble, rum—— ble,———
Roar, roar, roar, says the din - o - saur.———

Well the leaves fell down and the big trees died, They

lay — un-der wat-er and they nev - er dried,

Sand and mud — ov - er   top of them flowed, The

plants were crushed-by that heav - y — load. —

Squish, — squish, —   squish, —

Squish, squish, —   squish, —

Squeeze, squeeze, squeeze, All those   swamp-y trees. —

Ov - er   time — the   swamp-y trees,

Bur - ied   un - der the   an - cient seas,

Turned to peat — and   then to   coal,

Now they dig — it, It's the min - er's — goal. —

Dig   it, dig   it,   dig it, —

Dig   it, dig   it,   dig it, —

Roll, roll,   roll, All that good, black — coal. —

Discuss:

- whether fossil fuels are a renewable resource
- forms of energy that do not require the burning of fossil fuels
- how the burning of fossil fuels adds to the problem of acid precipitation
- find out how electricity is generated in your community; if coal is burned to produce electricity discuss this with your class and explore the relationship between electricity and acid precipitation

List some of the ways we can help the problem of acid rain (e.g. reduce our activities which require the burning of fossil fuels).

Students can create a diorama, poster, model, or bulletin board display of the complete cycle of fossil fuel formation, extraction, use, and the ways it might contribute to acid precipitation.

Measuring the acid in your rain

Students will examine the pH levels in rain or snow

Ensure that the students understand pH, acids and bases, the pH levels of acid rain and "normal" rain water.

Divide the students into groups and have them choose a nearby area where they will collect their rain or snow samples. Give each group 3 jars (baby food jars are good) and label them #1, #2, and #3 with the collection location and group member names. The jars should have been soaked in distilled water and kept in a plastic bag to avoid contamination.

When it rains have the students quickly put their jars out in their chosen sample locations. Try to collect at least 1 cm of rainwater. If you are using snow, carefully collect the snow in a plastic bag. Bring into the classroom and test it when the snow has melted.

Measure the pH of the samples, making sure to use a clean strip of pH paper for each sample. Record the pH levels, date, sample locations and sample number on an activity sheet.

Repeat this activity on the next rainy day. Results should be compared with the other groups. Which was the lowest pH recorded? Is this acid rain? Predict what the pH levels of rain in your area will be in 5, 10, and 15 years.

Trying to grow in acid rain

Students will examine how bean seeds respond to solutions with different levels of pH

Divide the class into groups and assign one solution to each group. Have the students make up the solutions if required. Solutions from "The acid test" can be used. Test the pH of the solutions and record on an activity sheet. Ensure that there is one group that uses distilled water and one that uses tap water for your control groups.

Place bean seeds between 4 sheets of paper towels. Wet the towels with the test solutions. Roll up the paper towels tightly. Place the towels in a plastic bag and label it with names and test solution.

Check the seeds every two days. Moisten when necessary. Record information about the seeds' growth on an activity sheet. Continue for one to two weeks.

Compare the growth of the seeds. How did acidic solutions affect the growth of the seeds? Which seeds grew the best? the worst? Discuss how acid precipitation might affect forests and crops and the animals and people dependent upon them.

The broken link

Students will understand how acid deposition can upset the food webs in aquatic and terrestrial ecosystems

Make up name tags for components of an ecosystem (e.g. for a terrestrial ecosystem: bacteria, soil, grass, earthworm, sowbug, tree, hawk, rabbit, lynx, bear, robin, sun, water, berry bush, human, etc.).

Distribute the name tags randomly. The students will each represent that component of the ecosystem. Students sit in a large circle; the circle represents the entire ecosystem. Discuss concepts such as food chains and ecosystems pointing out that all parts of the system are important just like a link in a chain. If one component is removed the others are affected.

Give a ball of string to the person representing an integral part of the chain (i.e. soil, grass, water, sun). Holding on to the string, that person passes the ball to a component that is connected to them. For example, grass may pass it to soil. Continue connecting items (e.g. soil to earthworm, earthworm to robin, robin to hawk) until a large "web" is formed and everyone is included.

Once you have the web, discuss what would happen if one component was affected by acid precipitation. For example, the water becomes very acidic and the food for fish die. The fish are affected as they lose their source of food. The bears who eat the fish from that stream may also lose a source of food.

Have the person representing water give their end of the string a tug. Who else feels it? If others feel it, they are somehow affected by the water becoming too acidic. If they feel a tug, they in turn should tug the string. It is likely that most members of the "ecosystem" will feel the tug. Discuss what is happening to the ecosystem. This activity can be done in a variety of units. Some other suggestions for situations: drought, severe deforestation, extinction of a species, pesticide use, soil contamination.

Relationships between members of the web do not have to be simply feeding chains. For example, a bird can be affected if a tree is cut because it loses its nesting habitat.

Alternative autos

Students will learn that by making decisions as consumers they can reduce the impact of their activities on the environment

Have the students choose an automobile advertisement. Try to get as many different vehicles as possible covered by the class. What type of vehicle are the ads trying to sell? What is emphasized in the ads? Is the car fast, attractive, practical, energy efficient. . . ? What are its strong and weak points?

Have each student present to the class the "selling points" of the vehicle chosen. They could pretend they are car salesman and are trying to sell this vehicle to the class.

Have students design a new car that is environmentally friendly. They can make a poster, advertisement, or model of this "car of the future".

Discuss some other "environmentally-friendly" types of transportation.

The maple leaf forever?

Students will examine how the maple leaf is used as a symbol to represent Canada, and will look at how acid rain is affecting maple forests

Discuss maple trees, listing all the things we get from maple trees and the places the maple leaf is used as a symbol of Canada (e.g. penny, crests, athletic uniforms, flag).

Read a newspaper article on the effect of acid rain on maple sugar bushes. In groups, brainstorm ideas of what might happen if maple forests died completely as a result of acid rain. The groups may need a bit of prompting to determine all the things that could potentially be affected. Here are a few ideas:
— maple sugar farmers would have no jobs
— we would use artificial syrup on our pancakes
— we might have to change our flag
— the price of pure maple syrup would increase
Accept all ideas and both good and bad effects. Write the ideas in the middle of a piece of paper, one per page. Then brainstorm ideas of what the consequences (positive and negative) would be if the effect actually occurred. The following graphic offers a beginning.

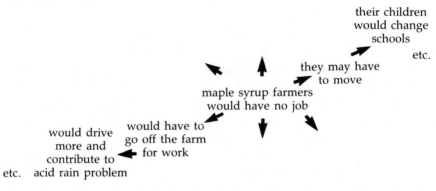

See how many causes and effects students can find for each consequence. Share the ideas of the groups. Post the sheets on a bulletin board. How many different ideas were there? What was one of the most creative ideas?

Visit a maple syrup farm if there is one in your area. Many good films and books exist on this topic if it is not possible to arrange a visit in your area.

See if there are any trees in your community that are suffering from the effects of acid rain. Here are some signs: branches at the top are bare, many branches have very few leaves, those leaves which remain are discolored, leaves begin to change color earlier in the autumn.

Pollution catchers

To use various methods to "catch" and observe air pollution

Try one or more of these methods to observe the air pollution in your area:

1. Have the students hang small pieces of white cloth in different locations (and at various heights) outside. After a few days examine the cloths with a magnifying glass. Have the students suggest the sources of the pollutants they have caught. You could very carefully hold a cloth behind the exhaust of a car to get a sample.
2. Place filter paper over the intake end of a vacuum cleaner. Students can take different air samples in different locations, changing the filter papers at each location and comparing all the different samples.
3. Students place small jars of water outside in various locations. They examine them the next day for floating materials and sediments. The water can be poured through coffee filters. What is left on the filters?
4. Place a piece of sticky tape, sticky side exposed, outdoors but protected from the weather, and a similar piece indoors. After a few days compare the two.

What did the class find out about the air quality where you live?

Research how environment officials test for air pollution in Canada. Have an official visit your class.

What are some effects of poor air quality on human health? Ask your doctor or health clinic.

Acid rain and you and me

Students will learn how acid precipitation can affect people in both direct and indirect ways

Read the poem "Acid Rain" by sean o huigin from *Scary Poems for Rotten Kids*, Black Moss Press and/or watch the NFB film, "Acid Rain" based on the poem. Discuss the poem or film.

Brainstorm ways that acid rain can affect people. Remember that acid rain can do damage to forests, crops, water, fish, human health, buildings and monuments. Include direct and indirect effects. Have students write poems or limericks about acid rain. Share them with the class and school.

In Los Angeles, the air pollution is so severe that the city is introducing some very stringent air emission control measures to reduce air pollutants by 80—90% by 2007. Air pollution is so bad in this city that there are times when people with respiratory troubles are told not to venture outside. Some measures L.A. will implement:

— gasoline powered vehicles will likely be banned from the roads by 2007; only clean-fueled vehicles (electric, methane) will be allowed
— ban sprays, outdoor barbecues, and gasoline-powered lawn mowers
— will encourage ride sharing
— will encourage people to work at home or to work an alternate work week (i.e. 10 hours a day for 4 days a week)
— may begin to televise university classes
— the paint industry, breweries, aerosol manufacturers, and bakeries would have to install equipment to reduce noxious emissions

Ask students to find articles on air pollution. What are some health effects of acid rain and other forms of air pollution? What can be done to alleviate the problem? In large cities where air pollution is a very serious problem how are city officials dealing with the problem? Ask students how they would combat air pollution problems in cities, if they were city officials.

Murder mystery at the lake

Students will compose and act out a murder mystery based on acid rain

Acid rain lends itself well to a murder mystery story. It looks innocent enough, but it does a lot of damage.

Have students work in groups to develop their play. Things they could consider: insects on the lake die out, fish stop breeding, birds that eat fish don't return to the lake, trees start to turn colors sooner, stone work on homes on a lakeshore start to erode. Who or what is causing it all?

Have the students act out the plays before another class. See if the audience knows what is causing all the damage. The audience should be left with the knowledge of what causes acid rain, and what they can do to help.

Understanding the greenhouse effect

Introduction

- The responsibility for greenhouse-gas emissions is uneven throughout the world: the West (15% of the world's population) is responsible for 46% of the emissions; USSR/eastern Europe (7% of the world's population—19%; Third World (78% of the world's population)—35%.

- Carbon dioxide levels in the atmosphere have risen steadily since the Industrial Revolution; they are presently rising at 3-4% per decade. This is a 25% increase in the last 300 years.

- Worldwide, humans pump approximately 4.5-5.5 billion tonnes of carbon into the atmosphere each year in the form of carbon dioxide, largely by burning coal, oil, gas, and wood.

- Each tree planted removes 4 kg of carbon dioxide from the air each year and converts it to oxygen.

When fossil fuels are burned they release gases into our atmosphere. Some of these gases, called greenhouse gases, act like the glass of a greenhouse and create a layer which traps the sun's heat in the atmosphere causing a warming of the earth's climate. This is commonly referred to as the greenhouse effect. A small layer of these gases is normal but the excess that is now present in our atmosphere causes abnormal levels of warming.

As the sun's rays travel to earth, they travel through a layer of carbon dioxide and the earth absorbs some of the heat. The earth reflects heat that is not absorbed as infrared radiation back into the atmosphere. Carbon dioxide is able to absorb infrared radiation and traps it in the earth's atmosphere rather than allowing it to escape into space. The amount of heat that stays near the surface is dependent on the amount of greenhouse gases, mainly carbon dioxide, in the atmosphere.

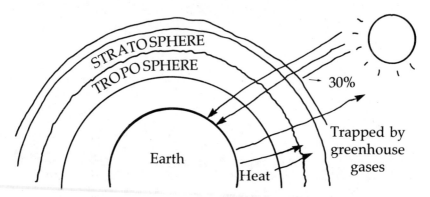

1. Solar energy enters the atmosphere and warms the earth.
2. The earth absorbs some of the sun's rays.
3. Heat wavelengths are reradiated off the earth's surface and are absorbed by a layer of greenhouse gases which send the heat back to earth. Some escape to the atmosphere.
4. As the greenhouse gas levels rise to a higher-than-normal level, more heat is captured in the lower atmosphere. Temperatures rise, affecting weather & climate.

The most common greenhouse gases are carbon dioxide, surface ozone, methane, nitrous oxide, and chloroflourocarbons (CFCs). CFCs are present in polystyrene* foam products including insulation, disposable cups and plates, some aerosols, and cooling systems of air conditioners and refrigerators.

Global warming

The greenhouse effect is believed to be causing an increase in the earth's temperature. Scientists have predicted that the build

---

*Styrofoam is a brand name. Products which are generically referred to as styrofoam are made of polystyrene foam.

up of greenhouse gases is likely to increase the Earth's surface temperature by between 1.5° and 4.5°C by the year 2030. This may not sound like too much, but the temperature difference between the last ice age (13 000 years ago) and warmer temperatures is just 5°C. While warmer temperatures may sound appealing if you live in northern climes, there are many problems associated with global warming. Higher temperatures could mean droughts turning productive land into desert. Temperature patterns could also change.

Scientists also think that a temperature rise could cause polar ice caps to melt resulting in a rise in the levels of the oceans by one to three metres. This would be potentially devastating for coastal communities. It is also likely that many plants and animals will be unable to adapt to the changes in temperature and climate.

To reduce the potential impact of global warming, the amount of greenhouse gases entering the atmosphere needs to be drastically reduced and forest clearing needs to be curtailed. To reduce the contribution from individuals we can all cut down on our use of fossil fuels and energy, try to use alternative forms of energy more often, eliminate our use of products that contain CFCs, and work to keep areas green with trees.

Ozone depletion

Imagine the ozone layer as being a giant sunscreen for the earth. Essentially, that is what it is. This layer protects the earth from the sun's harmful ultraviolet rays.

Ozone is found in the atmosphere up to 60 km from the earth surface but it is most dense 25-25 km up. There is actually quite a small amount of ozone in the atmosphere (if all of the ozone were collected and condensed it would cover the Earth's surface by only 3 mm), and therefore small changes in the amount of ozone translate into dramatic effects on Earth.

The Earth's ozone layer *is* getting thinner. In October 1987 scientists reported that the ozone layer over the Antarctic was depleted by 95%. A similar hole has recently been discovered over the Arctic.

The increase of ultraviolet light can threaten human and plant life. Ultraviolet light harms our eyes and immune systems, causes sunburn and snow blindness, can increase the occurrence of skin cancer, lowers the yields of food and timber crops and disrupts ocean food chains (plankton which grow in the ocean are important food for many invertebrates and fish and are important producers of oxygen).

The cause of ozone depletion has been linked to several chemicals which are used or produced by industry. Some include: chlorofluorocarbons (CFCs), nitrous oxide, and substances which contain chlorine, fluorine, and bromine. CFCs are the major contributor; they are used as propellants in aerosols, in refrigerator coolants, as foam-blowing agents in the plastic industry, and as electronic and dry-cleaning solvents.

Because CFCs are so stable (i.e. nontoxic, nonflammable, and non-biodegradable) they have become very popular for use over the last thirty years or so. But their stability is also why they are so dangerous. They can last in the atmosphere for more than one hundred years, "eating" away at the ozone.

In 1987, 40 countries signed the Montreal Protocol which called for the reduction of the world's output of CFCs by 20% by 1993 and another 30% by 1998.

To help prevent more ozone damage we can look for products which have a non-CFC label (food packaging, furniture foam, insulation, and electronic equipment), avoid the use of air-conditioners, and avoid dumping CFCs (CFCs can be recovered from refrigerators and car air conditioners).

Decoding the greenhouse effect

Students will learn how the greenhouse effect is contributing to global warming

Discuss global warming and the greenhouse effect with the class. Have students draw a diagram of how the greenhouse effect works. To explain the concept you may want to set up a terrarium in the classroom. Periodically take the temperature inside and outside the terrarium. Which is warmer? Why? How does this greenhouse compare to what is happening in the earth's atmosphere?

Discuss the types of things that might contribute to the greenhouse effect.

Using the secret code provided, or by creating a new one, have the students think of ways that they can help reduce their contribution to the greenhouse effect. They can swap their ideas with classmates, or put them on the board for the rest of the class to decode.

Global "releaf"

To discuss how planting trees can help to slow down the buildup of carbon dioxide in the atmosphere; to introduce the Global ReLeaf campaign of Friends of the Earth

To make a major impact on the reduction of greenhouse gas levels in the atmosphere major changes in industrialized countries must be made — a task over which few of us feel we have control. But planting trees and reducing our input of greenhouse gases is something we *all* can do.

Trees absorb carbon dioxide from the atmosphere for photosynthesis and therefore help to reduce the buildup of greenhouse gases. Trees also can help to improve the energy efficiency of buildings. Carefully placed trees can save on air-conditioning requirements in summer and can act as wind breaks and energy savers in winter.

The environmental group, Friends of the Earth, recently launched a program called "Global ReLeaf" which encourages citizens to plant trees — a positive action helping to reduce greenhouse gases.

Review how trees utilize carbon dioxide.

Photosynthesis equation:

CO_2 + H_2O + light = carbohydrate + oxygen + water (is actually CO_2 + $2H_2O$ $\underset{\substack{\text{green} \\ \text{plant}}}{\text{light}}$ (CH_2O) + O_2 + H_2O)

Review global warming and the greenhouse effect. What are some ways to alleviate the problem of global warming?

If the average white pine or maple tree takes one-third to one-half a tonne of carbon from the atmosphere and the average Canadian per capita production of carbon is four tonnes a year, how many trees must each person plant to become a "non-polluter"? (about 10 trees)

Transportation and the environment

To examine current transportation systems and the pros, cons, and alternatives

Using an activity sheet have the students list different kinds of transportation (walking, horses, bikes, a bus, cars, trucks, boats, trains, planes. . .). Once the list is complete, ask students to research:

— the materials and natural resources used to construct each transportation means
— the materials and resources necessary to operate and maintain the means of transportation
— the waste materials produced during operation
— the effects on the environment, both positive and negative

Organize a debate in which two groups discuss transportation methods, such as oil tanker vs. pipeline, freeway vs. subway or other form of mass transit, bike vs. car.

Have groups design methods of transit appropriate for your community. Then the groups can make a presentation to the class using illustrations, models, or diagrams.

Ask students to research the different methods of transportation that have been used since Canada was settled. How has the world changed since the car was introduced? Students should look at both environmental and social impacts. (Some ideas: urban design, distribution of population, pollution, relationships between people.)

There's more than one answer

To understand that there are many sides to an issue when you are dealing with environmental problems
    Copy the following roles onto separate index cards.

Logger
"I welcome the new mill. I will be able to get work cutting trees for the mill in the nearby forest."

Mill Worker
"I will be able to work again. I haven't had *steady* work in the three years since the old mill closed — and I have a family to support."

Member of "Citizens Against Global Warming"
"The logging of nearby forests and pollution from the mill will only contribute to global warming. If we *have* to build anything, let's build a paper recycling plant instead."

Biologist
"I have studied this caribou herd for 10 years now. I am very concerned how the logging will affect their population."

Tourist
"I love coming here every summer to hike in the nearby forest and canoe the clean lakes. Please preserve the area . . . it's one of the few wild lands left in our province."

Tour Operator
"I have worked hard the last two years to try and establish our town as a mecca for nature lovers — the mill will surely keep them away now."

Store Owner
"A new mill will mean more people living in our town. That's good news for me — maybe I can start on that expansion I've been dreaming about."

Teacher
"The mill will mean more families will be in town — so that's work for me! Also for the students already here, having their parents back at work will make their lives happier. I'm worried about health effects though; are there any I should be worried about?"

Ask eight students to draw a role play card; the remainder of the students can be members of the audience. More roles can be created.

The students will be part of a public hearing at a mock town council meeting. The discussion centres over whether a new pulp mill should be built in the town. There is fairly low unemployment in town but in the last few years more people have been visiting the area surrounding the town to get a glimpse of a rare species of caribou and to enjoy the wilderness.

Give participants five minutes to express their point of view. You can act as the mediator in the proceedings. Leave time for audience participation and debate between individuals.

Try to reach a group consensus. Is it possible? Was everyone happy with the decision or did some individuals have to compromise more than they wanted?

Auto lotto

To examine our society's relationship with automobiles

North Americans have a love affair with their cars. We know they are expensive, and most people know they harm the environment — but we continue to buy them. Our cities are designed for cars, not people!

Each year about ten million tonnes of air pollutants from cars are spewed into the atmosphere — that equals about 30% of all air pollutants in Canada. Pollutants include: nitrogen oxides, sulphur oxides, hydrocarbons, carbon monoxide, lead, and other metallic compounds.

Besides the air pollutants, the environmental impact of the car includes the enlargement of our roads and highways (there's always pressure to make more and make them wider), refineries and pipelines for fuel, and the sprawl of cities that are designed for cars.

Alternatives to the automobile or ideas to reduce its use include public transit, car pools, bicycles, walking.

As a class, record how many cars or trucks each family in your class has. Illustrate this on a bar graph.

Have a teacher or volunteer adult drive a few blocks (2-4 km) in an area with some traffic. How long did it take? Have an adult on a bike go the same distance. How long did it take? Which was faster? Was it faster by a large amount? Which was less stressful? less polluting? better exercise?

Ask students to give the advantages and disadvantages of riding a bike and of driving a car. How many people in their families ride a bike to school, work, or shopping?

Have students keep an auto-log of the times during a week their family vehicle was used. How many kilometres were travelled? Approximately how much gasoline was used? What did it cost? Were there alternative ways to make these trips? Were there advantages or disadvantages to an alternate form of travel?

Discuss the importance of cars in our society. How do we modify our environment to accommodate vehicles? Have students draw a map of a block around the school to see how many features there are for vehicles (e.g. roads, parking lots, parking spots on the streets, traffic lights).

To study what is involved in the use of alternate means of transportation, have students design a town or city that does not use cars.

Protecting our water supply

Introduction

- By the year 2000 it is estimated that the global consumption of water will be 10 times greater than it was in 1900. Many people, however, will still be without adequate water and sanitation.

- 80% of disease in developing countries is related to lack of safe drinking water and sanitation.

- A person needs five litres of water per day for drinking and cooking; each person needs 25-45 L of water each day to stay clean and healthy; people in North America use about 260 L of water each day.

- Most toilets use between 22-36 L per flush.

- Two-thirds of the world's households use a water source outside the home.

- Water haulers are usually women and in some countries women can spend as much as five hours a day collecting water for their family.

- About 70% of the human body is made up of water; each day our bodies lose about 2.5 L of water through respiration, perspiration, and excretion.

- Canadians use about 260 L of water daily for use in and around the home, another 6400 L is used on their behalf in industry, agriculture, and mining.

- How we use water in our homes:

toilet	45%
bathing and personal	28%
laundry and dishes	23%
drinking and cooking	4%

- Most items we use daily require the use of water in their production; for example:
  560 L water used/one Sunday newspaper
  120 L water used/500g of steel
  600 L water used/500g of aluminum

Of all water on our planet, 97% is salt water. Only 3% is fresh water, and most of that is frozen in the polar ice caps. Less than 1% of the Earth's water is actually available for our use.

The water we have is all that we have, we can't make anymore. It is continually cycling around us — sustaining all life. Just think, a drop of water you used to brush your teeth this morning may have been in Cleopatra's bath!

For something so vital to our survival, water is one of our most abused resources. We wash our windows with it, wash our cars, wash down chemical spills, clean paintbrushes, use it to make steel and plastic, *and* we drink it. The more we contaminate it, the more we have to treat it, try to clean it up; then we use it all over again.

In some countries water is plentiful, in others it is scarce and what there is is often polluted. Million of people die each year due to lack of water, lack of proper sanitary facilities, and waterborne diseases.

Even in countries where water seems plentiful, people are discovering that ground and surface waters are becoming contaminated by oil spills, chemical pesticides, street and soil run-off, leachates from dumps and landfills, industrial wastes, and sewage. Ground water is particularly vulnerable. It doesn't change much, so once it is polluted it remains polluted.

Many areas in North America also experience water shortages. The water supply in these areas is often groundwater and due to the sheer volume of its use, the land isn't given enough time to replenish its stocks. Demand exceeds the supply.

Animals often are signals to us of the plight of our water. In the Great Lakes many fish are found with tumors and abnormal growth. Beluga whales that live in the St. Lawrence River are becoming threatened because of toxic pollution in the waterway. Up to 1000 different chemicals have been detected in the Great Lakes! Are there any lakes or rivers in your community where you can no longer swim or fish?

Water pollution is something we all have a stake in and something we can all do something about. Conserving water (think of it as the water for the world, not just your community) and remembering that everything you put on the ground ends up in the water are good places to start.

Goin' round and round

To discuss how water is continually cycled in the environment

Review the activity "What goes up must come down", on page 66.

Discuss the sentence: Water evaporated in Alberta could be a drop of rain in Saskatchewan.

Have students write a poem or story or perform a puppet play about the life of a drop of water. Make sure to include where it is or what it is doing in each stage of the water cycle.

Brainstorm some ways we use water in its three states — liquid, solid, and gas.

Water — we need it to survive

Students will examine all the ways we use water in our lives and study the amount of water that is available for our use

Using an apple or a cantaloupe to represent the earth, you could ask the following questions and carve out the specific amount from the fruit.

- What percentage of the earth is water?   75%
  (cut a 25% wedge out of the apple, this represents land, the remaining piece represents water)

- What percentage of the earth's water is ocean?   97%
  (i.e. is not available for human consumption)
  (cut about 97% from the 75% wedge of "water" that remains

— this 97% represents the ocean. This leaves about 3% fresh water)

- What percentage of the earth's water is tied up in glaciers and icecaps?   2%
(cut 2/3 away from the small slice that remains, this represents water in glaciers and icecaps)

This last small slice (about 1%) is all that remains to represent the water that is available for human use.

Discuss this activity. Were students surprised by the amount of water available? Discuss that the distribution of fresh water throughout the world is also quite uneven. Some countries, such as Canada are water "rich". Others are not so lucky.

Discuss, "water, water everywhere and not a drop to drink".

Brainstorm ways in which we use water; include personal, agricultural, energy, and recreational uses.

Water bodies

To examine why people need clean water and what the water content of humans and some of our foods is

Have students predict the percentage of water in humans and in some of our foods. What is the consequence of dehydration in humans?

Cut open some fruits and vegetables and leave them exposed to the air. Study how they look each day. How do you know that they include water? Have the students record their guesses for the percentage of water in the food. Weigh the pieces of food daily. Leave them exposed until they are totally dry (this may take a while; if you can't wait, use a fruit dehydrator).

Brainstorm all the ways people *need* water. How much water do we need a day to survive? What would happen if we didn't get any water daily? How long can people survive without water?

Clean water is not always available in many places in the world. Many diseases are related to the absence of clean water and proper sanitation. In fact, 80% of the diseases in developing countries is related to poor drinking water and sanitation. Have students research one of these diseases and its relation to unclean water (some diseases: schistosomiasis, diarrhoea, dysentry, cholera, giardiasis, typhoid, hepatitis).

Water wise

To examine how much water we use in a day

Amount of water you need for basic survival:	5L
Amount of water used for:	
washing your face	7.5L
a bath	110L
a shower	75L
toilet flush	22L
getting a drink of water	1L
brushing teeth	1L
doing dishes	30L
washing the car	40L
cooking a meal	18L
using a washing machine	90L

Ask students to note all the activities done at home in one day that use water. They should calculate the amount of water used by them each day and by the family.

How does the daily consumption compare among classmates? to the Canadian average of 200-260 L? to a rural family in a developing country that relies on a stream several km away? (2-5L) to the amount of water needed for basic survival? (5L)

Discuss some of the ways water is wasted in the home.

Discuss some ways to reduce the amount of water used in the home. Some ideas: Dripping taps are often big culprits. Let a tap drip for a half hour. Collect the water. How much was collected? How much would be wasted if it dripped for a day? a week? Dripping taps usually only need a new washer at a cost of about 10 cents. Flushing toilets also uses a large amount. Displace water in a toilet tank using a plastic bottle or container filled with rocks. How much water is displaced? How much water is saved per flush? How much water would be saved in a family of four over a one week period?

Have students create a brochure with practical suggestions for wise water use to distribute to schoolmates, family, and the community.

Do you pay for water in your community? If you don't pay — should you? If people had to pay for water, do you think they would conserve it?

Water of the world

To study the uneven consumption of water in the world and to explain to the students that many people in the world are still without adequate water and sanitation

In two-thirds of the world's households, water is obtained from a source outside the home. The people who usually haul this water are women and they often spend a better part of their day hauling water for their family's use.

Lack of proper sanitation and adequate water is an ongoing fight in developing countries. The U.N. International Drinking Water Supply and Sanitation decade began to ensure water and sanitation for all by 1990. This target was never realized — in fact 300 million *more* people lack sanitation in 1990 than in 1980.

Household water consumption and, therefore, sanitation and health, is proportional to the distance from a water source. Consider these statistics on water use: households with dishwashers, washing machines, and sprinklers: 1000 L/person/day; households with piped water and taps: 100—350 L/person/day; households using a public hydrant in the street: 20—70 L/person/day; households depending on a stream or handpump several kilometres away: 2—5 L/person/day.

Discuss how easy it is for us to get water. To demonstrate this, ask one student to fetch a glass of water. Time how long it took. Discuss that, in many countries, the water source is outside the home and family members have to haul water each day. To emphasize this, calculate the distance a woman would have to spend hauling water in a part of Africa where the water source is two kilometres away. There are four people in her family. Each needs a minimum of 5 L per day (drinking and cooking) and 25 L more to stay clean. The most she can carry comfortably is 15 L at a time. In total how many kilometres would she have to go each day to get water? How long do you think that would take her? How does that compare to how quickly we get water?

Read the following article. How do the students think that having a new water well has changed the lives of the women and their families in Mwabungo? How has it changed the community?

Ask students where their water comes from. Where would they get water if it wasn't piped into their homes? Make a map of water sources near your community.

The long walk is over

The UN Decade is not all 'targets' and 'consultations' — it has changed some people's lives utterly.

Mwanaisha Mweropia, a 23-year-old mother of six from Mwabungo village in the Kenyan district of Kwale, used to make seven journeys a day to a well some distance away. There was always a line at the well, even at dawn, and the rule was that no-one might draw a second bucketful without joining the queue again. Everyone quarrelled and women with large families — which was most of them — were constantly tired. Mwanaisha coughed perpetually and had chronic chest problems.

In 1984 her life changed when the Kenyan Water for Health Organization (KWAHO) installed an Afridev handpump in Mwabungo — part of a special project to drill boreholes and install pumps in more than 100 local communities. Rainfall in this arid coastal area is seasonal and most streams and traditional wells dry up. Women were trekking long distances to dig in dry riverbeds. The picture is a familiar one in Africa where 60 per cent of women engage in grinding strain and hours of labour to produce a few miserable bucketfuls of water — which are often unsafe to drink.

Not only is the Afridev hand-pump much closer to Mwanaisha's home and far less onerous to operate but the water is safe and her cough and chest pains have disappeared. The local KWAHO community worker, Mwanauba Omar, says that all water-related disease has declined.

The striking feature of KWAHO's programme, which has attracted much international attention during the Water Decade, is the degree to which it is focussed on women. The organization was inspired by women, is mostly run by women, and has fully involved women in the villages.

The Water Ministry drills the boreholes, which at up to 50,000 shillings ($3,125) each are the most expensive part of the pumps. KWAHO gives the pumps and knits people together. Each community collects money — a shilling (six cents) a week per family — for repairs and replacements. To Mwanaisha Mweropia it is a small price to pay for a better, healthier life.

Winnie Ogana/Panos
SOURCE: The New Internationalist

To demonstrate how our behavior would change if we had a limited water supply (or it was not easily accessible) distribute "water trip tickets". Each student should be given a stack of water tickets that must last them one week. Each time they use water they have to relinqiush a ticket. Did they think twice about using water? Did they only use it if necessary?

Have students research programs that are trying to establish clean water for people in the world. International aid organizations, the United Nations, and local churches may be good places to start the research.

Water conservation plans

To develop a water budget plan for home

Brainstorm ways to conserve water. Have students develop a plan for conserving water in their homes. Could all the ideas be implemented at once? Would some ideas take more planning? Would some take a bit of time to convince the family to partici-pate? Have students implement their plans. Discuss the projects. Were families cooperative? Were some of the ideas harder to implement than others?

Watching the river run

To look at our historical and present-day use of rivers

Have students research the historical use of rivers in Canada, paying particular attention to use by native peoples and the fur brigades. Why might the fur brigades, or voyageurs, be referred to as the truck drivers from our past? "En Roulant Ma Boule" is one song that the voyageurs might have sung as they paddled. The class can learn the song.

What do we use rivers for now? Ideas: recreation, transporta-tion, hydroelectricity, sewage, drinking water.

Have students brainstorm some positive and negative conse-quences of our activities on rivers. What alternatives are there?

Hydroelectric dams, in particular, can radically change the environment due to massive flooding. Demonstrate how a hydroelectric dam works. Make a dam from plasticine and fill it with water. Water is stored behind the dam and when it is released the momentum of the falling water is used to create elec-tricity. Poke a pencil hole in the dam. Put a pinwheel in the water stream to represent a turbine. What happens to the land upstream of a dam? What happens to communities upstream? to wildlife? to forests?

Ask students to research areas of your province that have major dam projects. How has the dam affected these areas (both the environment and the people)?

There are organizations in Canada (Canadian Heritage Rivers) and the United States (Wild and Scenic Rivers) that work to pre-serve rivers. Contact one of these groups to find out if there is a specially recognized river near your community. Why has it been recognized?

Take a field trip to a hydroelectric dam to see how it operates.

Take a field trip to a nearby river. Sit on the banks and observe all the activity that is going on around the river. Students can write a poem about their experience at the river.

Examine a good map of a river near your community. Discuss the watershed of this river (the area drained by streams, creeks, and lakes into the river). What might happen if some of the valleys leading into the river were clear cut? If the land near the river was sprayed by pesticides?

Water fights

To demonstrate that there is often competition over the use of a body of water

There is often competition for available, useful water near communities. Hold a mock town meeting in your class where members of the community debate the use of a local lake. Community representatives could be: farmers (want it for irrigation), commercial fishermen, sports fishermen, native fishermen, recreational boaters/water skiers, tour boat operators, canoeists, municipal drinking water officials (want it for a reservoir), conservationists (want restricted use; protect the area for wildlife).

Have the representatives prepare a list of reasons why they should be able to use the lake for their purpose. Can more than one interest be accommodated? Can the town council come to a consensus on how the lake should be used?

Life in a watery world

To observe creatures that live in and around streams or lakes

Visit a local stream or lake. Pick a quiet spot on the banks and observe the area. Have students describe the area using as many senses as possible. How does it look, smell, sound. . . ? What types of plants are growing nearby? Are there any plants growing in the water? What animals live on top of the water? in or near the water?

Take a closer look at what lives *in* the water. Using dip nets and turkey basters, students should take water samples and study the creatures in the water. What did they see? They can draw and describe some of the water creatures. Do any fish live in the water? What kinds? What do they eat?

Students can write a poem or story, create a play, create a song or dance about the activities around the stream or lake.

The class can adopt the stream or lake, and visit it regularly, study its changes, conduct clean-ups, and take part in enhancement programs.

Water pollution

To observe how adding some things to water can pollute it, and to research different forms of water management

Many detergents contain nutrients such as phosphates. When these phosphates enter rivers and lakes they provide an extra boost of nutrients to the algae growing there. Consequently "algal blooms" occur. It doesn't sound so bad, but the algae grow and spread throughout the water, use up the valuable oxygen, and crowd out other plants. Consequently the aquatic life dies.

Fill two large jars or fish bowls with water from a nearby stream or lake, and place them in a sunny spot. Have the class monitor them daily for the growth of algae. Once the algae is growing add a small amount of phosphate detergent to one of the bowls. Add a bit more detergent each day. Have students describe what happens to the algae in this bowl. If you have space, use a third bowl and add pure soap to it. Why do environmental groups recommend that we use soap rather than detergent?

Brainstorm some other pollutants that can be put into the water. What are the effects of these pollutants on the water? Some ideas: industrial wastes, pesticides, fertilizers, gas, oil, thermal pollution (water that is used to cool power plants — it is often returned to its source warmer than normal).

What is the water management plan in your community? Visit a sewage treatment facility or have a speaker come and visit your class.

Is drinking water fluoridated in your community? What are the pros and cons to fluoridation? Have a dentist speak to your class about fluoridation.

Conserving energy

Introduction

- Canada's energy consumption is the highest in the world.

- 19% of Canada's energy is supplied by solar, wind, water, geothermal, and biomass resources (i.e. renewable sources). If hydroelectric projects are omitted, only 7% of Canada's energy is from renewable sources.

- Each year the average Canadian uses 18 000 kg of petroleum, coal, natural gas, and uranium to produce goods, fuel, and heat for homes, cars, and industrial materials.

- Energy savings for recycled materials rather than making materials from raw resources: paper 23-70%, steel 47-75%, aluminum 95%, copper 90%.

- If everyone in the United States turned down their thermostat by 6°F, 500 000 barrels of oil per day would be saved.

Energy is the capacity to do work. It can be anything doing the work — people, animals, or machines. Forms of energy used in Canada are varied and include fossil fuels (oil, natural gas, and coal). hydroelectric, nuclear, wood, solar, and wind.

Traditionally, fossil fuels and wood have been used to supply our energy needs but overuse of these non-renewable resources have resulted in shortages, higher prices, and environmental problems. To attempt to deal with these problems, alternative sources of energy are continually being researched and Canadians are learning to become more energy efficient.

Most energy resources, both renewable and non-renewable, have both positive and negative qualities. Economics and environmental problems are by and large the two criteria examined when choosing a source for energy.

Electricity is a secondary energy resource. It is manufactured from a variety of primary energy resources including water, coal, nuclear energy (uranium), oil, and solar power. The primary energy resources used to generate electricity in Canada vary but most provinces have a predominant source that they use.

Canada's current energy consumption is the highest per capita in the world. Our abundance of natural resources (particularly coal and water) may have something to do with our enthusiastic overconsumption — we've never really had to worry. This attitude however, is changing. Non-renewable resources won't last forever, we can't continue to dam all our free-flowing rivers for hydroelectric power, and acid rain and global warming are serious threats to our planet. Our high levels of energy consumption must be curtailed. Contrary to a widely held belief, curtailing consumption will not cause great hardship. We just need to reassess our needs and wants and put to rest the assumption that energy is "clean" and endless in supply. This unit introduces the forms of energy available, how we use energy, and how we can conserve it.

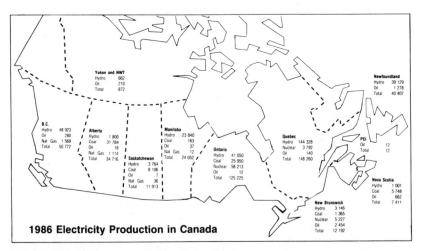

Map of Canada's use of energy resources used for the generation of electricity in 1986, measured in gigawatthours (GWh) or millions of kilowatthours.

Source: *Nuclear Facts*

There's energy all around us

To introduce different forms of energy that are available for use

Students can complete the word search of the types of energy sources that are available. Use the glossary of energy items to briefly discuss as a class any forms of energy with which the students are unfamiliar.

Have the students choose an energy source about which they would like to learn more. Try to have most of the energy sources covered by someone in the class. Students should describe in a short paragraph and a drawing how their energy source works.

Discover what sources of energy are used in your province. Trace the outline of Canada from an atlas. Have students use symbols to identify locations of energy sources such as oil, coal, or gas fields, hydroelectric plants (dams), nuclear power plants, coal, oil, or gas power plants, oil sands, oil or gas pipelines. Provincial/federal energy ministries are good sources for information.

Energy Glossary

biomass   sources of energy that come from plant and animal matter (include: trees; crops, such as wheat and corn, that can be made into alcohol; wastes (manure); basically, it is energy that is gained from something that was once alive

charcoal   a black, carbon-containing material that is prepared by heating wood in a container where there is no air

coal   a solid, black material which is formed by the decomposition of plant material in the absence of air; when it is burned it gives off heat; it is widely used as a fuel

crude oil   a black liquid formed from animal and plant material which collected at the bottom of ancient shallow seas

electricity   a form of energy where coal, water, oil, gas, or nuclear energy forms are converted into usable energy by people

food   a source of energy for animals and people

gasoline   a colorless liquid that burns quickly and produces energy; produced after crude oil (petroleum) or natural gas is refined geothermal   energy produced by the internal heat of the earth; usually is steam, hot water, hot rocks, or volcanic molten rock

human power   using our bodies to work

hydroelectricity   electricity generated from falling water; dams are built across rivers and water is collected in a reservoir; the energy of the released falling water turns turbines and generates electricity; water may also come from natural sources such as waterfalls that do not require damming

methane   a colorless, odorless, flammable gas

natural gas   colorless, odorless, highly flammable gas formed naturally in the earth; is used as a fuel

nuclear   energy produced by capturing the power released by the splitting of an atom (atomic energy)

ocean currents   energy obtained by harnessing the energy produced by ocean currents

oil sands   coarse-grained rock (i.e. sandstone) that contains deposits of petroleum

solar   energy produced from the radiation of the sun; the sun's energy is captured in solar panels and can be used for heat or turned into electric energy and stored to be used later

tar sands   deposits of sand or sandstone containing tarlike bitumen (coal-like substance); mainly found along the Athabasca River in Alberta

tidal power   energy produced by the falling and rising of ocean tides

wave power   energy obtained by harnessing the energy produced by ocean waves

wind energy   produced by wind turning wind mills; the energy can be used directly or stored in batteries for later use

wood   produced by a tree converting the sun's energy during photosynthesis; when trees are burned they release energy as heat

Word Search

c	e	o	n	e	d	t	a	g	r	o
r	t	s	l	a	o	c	r	a	h	c
u	b	g	d	o	o	w	g	s	y	e
d	e	a	b	t	f	e	t	b	d	a
e	m	t	i	d	a	l	h	l	r	n
o	d	c	o	a	l	o	m	i	o	c
i	i	o	m	e	t	h	a	n	e	v
l	l	l	a	r	q	e	c	e	l	r
k	a	x	s	t	v	u	f	s	e	r
e	m	c	s	a	l	k	o	a	c	e
s	r	s	w	e	n	d	i	g	t	n
d	e	b	p	r	v	d	l	l	r	t
n	h	v	m	a	n	s	s	a	i	s
a	t	p	d	e	o	g	a	r	c	b
s	o	x	c	l	g	x	n	v	i	n
r	e	l	a	c	t	h	d	t	t	o
a	g	r	b	u	m	i	s	a	y	l
t	j	g	d	n	i	w	o	n	j	z

Find the following types of energy:

They can be : ↑ ↓ → ← ↗ ↓ ↖ ↓

biomass	geothermal	oil sands
charcoal	human power	solar
coal	hydroelectricty	tar sands
crude oil	methane	tidal
electricity	natural gas	wave
food	nuclear	wind
gasoline	ocean currents	wood

Two types of energy

To define energy and to distinguish between renewable and non-renewable forms of energy

Energy is the ability to do work. We all use energy in various forms every day. Students should understand that when they walk, run, or ride their bikes they are using physical energy that has been fueled by food.

Non-renewable resources are just that — once they're gone, they're gone. Non-renewable resources include fossil fuels: coal, oil, and natural gas. These resources were created over many millions of years and they are still being formed underground but will take many millions of years to replace.

For these resources to be used, they must be burned. This produces gases that cannot be reused. As well, the gases contribute to air pollution problems including acid rain and global warming. Nuclear energy that is created by using uranium is also non-renewable.

Renewable energy comes from resources that will always be available: sun, wind, and water. These energy sources can also be used to make electricity, and to heat homes and water but their supply is replaceable. Geothermal energy and biomass energy are also renewable energy sources, but are not as commonly used.

Discuss as a class the difference between non-renewable and renewable resources. Brainstorm sources of renewable and non-renewable energy.

Have each student research one form of renewable or non-renewable energy, listing the pros and cons of the energy source. The research should consider if the source is readily available, what is practical for your community (obviously tidal power isn't appropriate for Regina), the cost, and the effects on the environment. (Teachers should note that just because a source is renewable it doesn't mean there are no environmental effects. Hydro-electric dams result in massive areas being flooded and there are concerns with reactor safety and waste disposal from nuclear power plants.)

Students' research can be combined in a poster presentation.

Energy-users

To help students understand that we use energy and natural resources every day

Brainstorm all the activities we do during the day using action verbs (e.g. eating, drawing, writing, reading, washing). As a class, list the materials used to perform each activity. List the origin of these materials. List the energy required to perform these activities.

An example could be writing as the activity, paper and pencils as materials used, trees, wood, and lead as the origins of the materials, and human energy as the energy required to perform the activity.

Discuss whether students were surprised by the amount of energy and natural resources they used. Were there some activities that did not require energy? did not require natural resources? What resources were used most often? Are these sources renewable or non-renewable?

Electricity in your home

To calculate how much energy home appliances demand and how much electricity they use in the home over the course of a day

Electric energy used in the home is measured in kilowatt hours (1 kilowatt = 1000 watts). Total energy used is measured by the energy meter located on the outside of a house. Electric appliances are usually marked on the outside with the wattage (electricity demand) that they require.

Explain that the electric demand of an appliance is called the wattage.

Have students fill in an activity sheet using five appliances that are common in the home or school. They can list the wattage of each, and then convert watts to kilowatts (divide watts by 1000). Students estimate how many hours a day these appliances are used, and then calculate the kilowatt hours (multiply by hours).

Ask students to calculate the cost of using these appliances. If electricity costs 5 cents per kilowatt hour, what was the price of electricity for one day, week, month, year?

Using the following example, have students practise reading electrical meters. A few tips for you to note:

- most residential meters have 5 dials, but some have 4
- the meters are read in kilowatt hours
- the dials are read from left to right
- each dial rotates in the opposite direction to the one beside it
- when the pointer is between two digits, the smaller number is read

2 4 8 4 1 kW·h

Give students two sets of dials, and have them read their own electricity meter for two successive days. They can calculate the kilowatt hours used, and list the electrical appliances that were used in those two days. As a class, compare results. Some households will have higher readings than others. Why? How many people are in each home? Are the homes large or small?

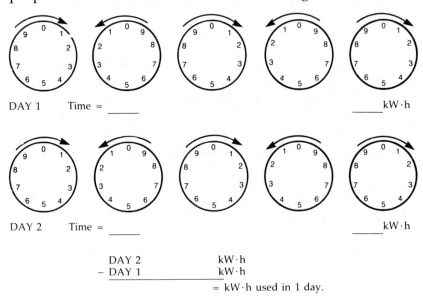

DAY 1   Time = _____   _____ kW·h

DAY 2   Time = _____   _____ kW·h

DAY 2	kW·h
– DAY 1	kW·h
= kW·h used in 1 day.	

Have the students record the readings for another week when the family tries to conserve energy. Is there a change?

If possible, take readings from your school's electricity meter. Record the meter for a week. Speculate why the amount used would fluctuate (colder/warmer temperatures, weekend).

The global powerhouse

Students should understand that the sun is the ultimate source of energy

Of all of the sun's energy that reaches the earth's atmosphere, 30% is reflected back into space, 47% is absorbed by the earth's surface and is converted to heat energy, 23% drives the water cycle. Less than 1% drives winds and ocean currents and 0.02% is captured by plants and provides the world's food energy, and produces the stored fossil-fuel energy. For these reasons it is fair to say that the sun is the primary source of all energy on earth.

How the sun is tied into all sources of energy:

Solar — directly from the sun

Wind — wind is caused by the unequal heating of the earth by the sun

Water — without the sun, the water cycle would not occur

Hydro-electricity — requires water to work

Fossil fuels — (coal, oil, natural gas) — ancient plants and animals required the sun to grow; fossil fuels are often referred to as "buried sunshine".

As a class discuss how all sources of energy are ultimately reliant on the sun. Brainstorm all the things we use that rely on the sun. Looking around your classroom will give you lots of ideas (plants, book, people. . .). Imagine what the world would be like without the sun. Would this be possible?

Do an experiment to see how solar panels work. Use two large dishpans or other large flat containers. Line one pan with black paint, paper, or a garbage bag. Fill both pans with water. Cover the pans with glass or clear plastic. Take the air and water temperatures in each container every hour or so. What happened?

Solar panels work almost exactly like the lined pan in this experiment. Solar collectors look like boxes covered with glass.

The dark colored metal plates inside the boxes absorb sunlight and change it into heat. Water pipes flow through the boxes and are warmed by the heat collected.

Make a solar cooker. This reflective cooker reflects the sun's rays into a small area and enables you to cook in it.

If you don't have the time to make a solar cooker you might want to test the saying, "it's hot enough to fry an egg on the sidewalk!" Sidewalks do a good job of holding solar heat — have fun trying this, but wait for a hot, hot day. Try frying one egg right on the sidewalk, one in a cast iron frying pan without a lid, and another in a cast iron frying pan covered in glass or plexiglass. (Leave the pans out in the sun for awhile before you try to fry). Which method worked best?

Keeping an energy account

Students will learn the difference between renewable and non-renewable resources and how they affect our environment; basic banking methods will also be learned

Review renewable and non-renewable resources and the pros and cons of both types.

Design an Energy Bank activity sheet. Decide as a class which actions will be credits (those which use no or small amounts of non-renewable resources) and debits (those which may adversely affect the environment). Post the list of credits and debits in the classroom. Arbitrarily assign point values for each action.
e.g. rode my bike to school instead of getting Mom to drive me = credit of 100 points
e.g. left the TV on when I went out for awhile = debit of 125 points
e.g. ran the water while I brushed my teeth = debit of 50 points. Items can be added to the list as the activity progresses.

Each student begins with 100 points and throughout the week calculates the credits and debits for his or her energy bank.

Who has the biggest bank account at the end of a week? Did they try hard to conserve energy? Were there other reasons why they were able to have such a big balance?

Share your ideas for energy conservation with your school. Make a giant paper chain with an idea for an easy way to save energy and help the environment written on each link. Challenge other classes. How long a chain can be made?

Alternatives

To examine the things that we use to make our lives easier and to consider the alternatives

In small groups have the students search through catalogues to find some of the tools that we use to make our lives "easier". They do not just have to be home appliances; escalators, typewriters, copy machines, etc. can be included.

These items are listed one per index card. When at least 20 cards are prepared, the stack is swapped with another group.

Still in the groups, one person draws one of the cards. The item is read out and the person on the right should shout out an alternative item that would do the same job, but doesn't use power to run. Some examples might be vacuum cleaner—broom, escalator—stairs, electric can opener—manual can opener, food processor—knife, color TV—a book, electric toothbrush—manual toothbrush, automobile—bike or walking.

Once an alternative has been suggested, as a group, discuss the pros and cons of both the product and its alternative.

Continue through the cards. Most of these new tools have been developed to make our lives easier. Have they?

Individually have the students choose one of the items identified. They can find an advertisement for this item in a newspaper, magazine, or catalogue. What things does the ad emphasize? Is it quick, easier, stylish. . . ? Then students can write and illustrate an advertisement for the alternative product or produce a TV or radio advertisement. Which features of the product did they emphasize?

The class could watch the film: "This Is A Recorded Message" that looks at the role of advertising in influencing our habits as consumers.

Discuss how pioneers performed some of the tasks for which there are now machines. If possible, visit a museum to see some of these earlier implements.

The night the lights went out

To imagine what a day would be like if there was no electricity
Read the following scenario to the class.

It is 6 p.m. on a cold, stormy Tuesday evening in November. You have just sat down to eat dinner with your family when all the power goes off. You fumble around the house and find your transistor radio (battery powered of course!). After listening for awhile you discover that the power is off all over town and cannot be restored until the following morning around 10 a.m. What would you do?

Ask students to write down all the tasks they would normally do that require electricity from 6 p.m. to 10 a.m. They should think about alternate ways to perform these tasks. How would they see, keep warm, cook, keep food cold? Discuss the ideas generated by the students.

Ask students to plan a menu of nutritious meals for the day when the power was off.

Have students prepare a plan for their home to deal with a day of power failure. They can devise what could be put in a "Power Failure Kit" (battery-powered radio, candles, food, blankets, etc.). Where would be the best place to put this kit?

Fuel for people

To examine simple food chains and how food is the fuel that powers people
Review herbivores, carnivores, omnivores and food chains.

Food is the fuel that all animals need to fuel their bodies and create energy. Different animals have different food needs. Some eat meat only (carnivores), some eat plants only (herbivores), and some eat both (omnivores). Other animals, called scavengers, eat plants and animals when they are dead. Review these categories with the students. Ask them in which category they are. Ask them what would happen if there were no scavengers.

Review with the students the fact that all these types of animals are needed in our environment and that they live together in what are called "ecosystems". All parts of the ecosystem are connected in food chains or food webs. Give students an example of a simple food chain such as:

$$grass \rightarrow grasshopper \rightarrow frog \rightarrow snake$$

Have students provide another example of a simple food chain. Ask them if food chains could exist without the sun, and why or why not.

Have students list what they had for lunch. Make food chain mobiles for each item in their lunch, using pictures from magazines or by drawing the components of the food chain; e.g. roast beef (water and sun → grass → cattle → meat), bread (water and sun → wheat → flour → bread) and milk (water and sun → grass → cow → milk). Use a hanger or sticks to hang the pictures.

The class could watch "Nature's Food Chain" (NFB #1 0177 148) in which all the parts and their function in food chains are explained.

As a class discuss food pyramids. As you move from link to link in the food chain more and more energy is lost. If you look at it one way, plants are really the *only* food on earth. Without them, no other animals would be able to exist. Plants take the energy from the sun, photosynthesize and create food. The higher up you go on a food chain, the more energy is lost. For example, a field of grass may feed 1000 grasshoppers, which may feed 100 frogs, which may feed only 10 snakes.

To illustrate this to the class create a food pyramid. It is preferable to do this activity on a soft lawn.

Food Pyramids

A food pyramid consists of plants, herbivores, carnivores, and scavengers (in this activity, scavengers are not included but can be discussed at the end). Food or energy pyramids illustrate the number of lifeforms at each level of a food chain. Energy is transferred from one level to another in the pyramid.

Give each student a slip of paper and have them write down an animal or plant found in the area.

Ask the class where the food pyramid will get its energy (the sun). What uses the sun's energy (plants). Have all those students who chose to be plants kneel down in a line. (At this point don't be too concerned if not too many students have chosen to be plants).

What eats the plants? Have all the herbivores stand in a row behind the plants.

What eats the herbivores? Have all the carnivores stand in a row behind the herbivores.

Have the class try to build a stable pyramid with the plants on the bottom, then the herbivores, then the carnivores. Usually for the first round it will be impossible to make a stable pyramid as more children prefer to be animals than plants.

Try to build a new pyramid. Have the majority of the students become plants (e.g. grass) to build a stable bottom for the pyramid. Then have the herbivores (e.g. mice) get on the backs of the plants. Then the carnivores (e.g. an owl) — there should only be one or two. How long can they keep the pyramid stable? Once everyone has settled down, review the concept of the food pyramid.

Once the students understand food pyramids, begin a discussion of energy loss between the levels of the food chain or pyramid and the inefficiency (energy and resources-wise) of consuming large amounts of meat.

As energy moves from the sun to plants to animals much of it is lost. An animal only gains 10% of the energy of the plant it eats; 90% is lost to heat or is never digested. Therefore it is much more energy efficient and environmentally sound to eat lower on the food chain.

For example, a very large amount of grain is used to feed animals so that we can eat them later. For every 8 kg of grain and soybeans fed to beef cattle, we get back only 500g as meat on our plates. Put in other terms, that means that the grain needed to provide a family of four with just one serving of hamburgers could feed someone in a developing country for a week. In the United States it is estimated that the livestock population consumes enough grains and soybeans to feed over five times the entire human population of the country.

Brainstorm some ideas why people might become vegetarians. (Most students will think of animal welfare but few will think of the environment). Have a discussion of the above points. Divide the class into small groups and have them investigate the food habits of people who are vegetarians. Create a vegetarian menu for a meal. If you have the facilities, create the meal.

Conserver city

To design a city that is energy efficient, environmentally sound, and uses resources wisely

Have the students imagine they are engineers, waste management consultants, transportation experts, architects, or city planners. Divide them into small groups to devise a plan for an environmentally-sound and energy efficient city of the future.

Things to consider:
transportation systems
homes
parks
hospitals
work places
waste management strategies
water sources
energy sources

A model or large poster of the energy efficient city could be produced.

Research the history of your community. What were the sources of energy and water in the early community. What were the transportation systems like? What was the system for waste management?

Energy monsters

To demonstrate an understanding of ways to conserve energy

In groups, students can create skits, radio plays, or a puppet play showing the transformation of a person (or family or creature) from an ''energy-monster'' to an ''energy-conserver''. They should show the ways to conserve water, energy, and resources. Video or record the plays or the class can perform for the school.

An ''energy-monster'' could be created in art class.

111

A positive response

After your students have participated in some of the activities in this book, see how they respond to comments such as the following.

"I don't contribute to the greenhouse effect or any other environmental problem".

"I hear about problems in the environment but none of them affects me."

"I like my life the way it is. If I start getting concerned about environmental problems my lifestyle won't be as good."

"It's too hard to cut back and reduce — what I do isn't going to help anyways."

"It's too depressing — I just don't want to think about it".

"What if I go to all this trouble to change and other people don't?"

"I'll just wait for the government to do something."

Directory of organizations

If you would like more information about the environmental issues in *The Green Classroom*, here are a few of the organizations that can provide resource material.

Atmospheric Environment Service,
Canadian Climate Centre,
4905 Dufferin Street,
Downsview, Ontario
M3H 5T5.
(416) 739-3423

Canadian Arctic Resources Committee,
46 Elgin Street,
Ottawa, Ontario,
K1P 5K6.
(613) 236-7379

Canadian Coalition on Acid Rain,
112 St. Clair Avenue West,
Toronto, Ontario,
M4V 2Y3.
(416) 968-2135

Canadian Coalition for Nuclear Responsibility
P.O. Box 236 Snowdon,
Montreal, Quebec,
H3X 3T4.
(514) 489-2665

Canadian Environmental Defense Fund,
347 College Street,
Suite 301,
Toronto, Ontario,
M5T 2V8.
(416) 323-9521

Canadian Environmental Network,
P.O. Box 1289,
Station B,
Ottawa, Ontario,
K1P 5R3.
(613) 563-2078.

Canadian Nature Federation,
453 Sussex Drive,
Ottawa, Ontario,
K1N 6Z4.
(613) 238-6154

Canadian Parks and Wilderness Society,
Suite 1150,
160 Bloor Street East,
Toronto, Ontario,
M4W 9Z9.

Canadian Wildlife Federation,
1673 Carling Avenue,
Ottawa, Ontario,
K2A 3Z1.
(613) 725-2191

Climate Institute,
316 Pennsylvania Avenue,
S.E.,
Suite 403,
Washington, D.C.,
20003.
(202) 547-0104

Ducks Unlimited Canada,
1190 Waverly Street,
Winnipeg, Manitoba,
R3T 2E2.
(204) 477-1760

Energy, Mines and Resources,
Canada,
Communications Branch,
580 Booth Street,
Ottawa, Ontario,
K1A 0E4.

Energy Probe,
225 Brunswick Street,
Toronto, Ontario,
M5S 2M6.
(416) 978-7014

Environment Canada,
Environment Protection
Service,
25 St. Clair Avenue East,
6th Floor,
Toronto, Ontario,
M4T 1M2.

Friends of the Earth,
251 Laurier Avenue West,
Ottawa, Ontario,
K1P 5J6.
(613) 230-3352

Friends of the Rainforest,
Department of Biology,
Carlton University,
Ottawa, Ontario,
K1S 5B6.

Global Greenhouse Network
(International),
c/o Jeremy Rifkin,
1130 17th Street N.W.,
Suite 630,
Washington, D.C.,
20036.
(202) 466-2823

Green Teacher,
95 Robert Street,
Toronto, Ontario,
M5S 2K5.
(416) 960-1244

Greenpeace Canada,
2623 West 4th Avenue,
Vancouver, British
Columbia,
V6K 1P8.
(604) 736-0321

Outdoors Unlittered,
45,9912-106 Street,
Edmonton, Alberta,
T5K 1C5.
(403) 429-0517

Pollution Probe Foundation,
12 Madison Avenue,
Toronto, Ontario,
M5R 1S1.
(416) 926-1907

Society, Environment and Energy Development Studies Foundation (SEEDS),
440-01069 104th Street,
Edmonton, Alberta,
T6J 5C1.
(403) 424-0971

The Acid Rain Foundation,
1410 Varsity Drive,
Raleigh, North Carolina,
27606.
(919) 828-9443

The Environmentally Sound Packaging Coalition,
2150 Maple Street,
Vancouver, British
Columbia,
V6J 3T3
(604) 736-3644

Western Canada Wilderness Committee,
20 Water Street,
Vancouver, British
Columbia,
V6B 1A4.

World Wildlife Fund Canada,
50 St. Clair Avenue East,
Suite 201,
Toronto, Ontario,
M5T 1N5.
(416) 923-8173

25 things your school can do to help

1. Encourage walking, cycling, carpooling or public transport for students and teachers. Designate one day a week a car-free day.
2. Recycle beverage containers from the lunchroom and staffroom. Use the money for school activities.
3. Hold a litter-drive to clean up the playground, school yard or neighborhood.
4. Adopt a local stream or river to study it, clean up and enhance if necessary.
5. Turn off the classroom, staffroom and gymnasium lights when not in use. Try to use natural light as much as possible.
6. Replace regular incandescent lightbulbs with the new compact fluorescent bulbs on the market. They may be more expensive but they last 10-13 times as long.
7. If your school yard has pesticides applied to it ask the school board to consider using safe alternatives — if it needs to be done at all.
8. Use both sides of note paper.
9. Make scrap paper pads and place them by all of the phones in the school and in the staffroom.
10. Reduce waste at the photocopier. Photocopy on both sides.
11. Use water-based paints, markers and glue.
12. Set aside part of your school's playground and develop a ''nature area''. Plant trees, grass, flowers, a vegetable garden and fruit trees, add ponds and bird feeders! Donate vegetables to families in need.
13. Purchase paper products (writing paper, computer paper, paper towels, toilet paper) made out of recycled paper.

14. Start a recycling program.
15. Encourage field trips to local parks or nature centres.
16. Limit the amount of disposable items used in the school.
17. Encourage students and staff to bring "garbage-free" lunches.
18. Start a school compost pile with scraps from the lunchroom, staffroom and yard clippings. Use the compost for a school garden or donate it to a local gardener.
19. Use environmentally-friendly cleaning products.
20. Grow plants in classrooms, staffrooms, offices and hallways.
21. Start an environment club.
22. Adopt a policy to make the school energy efficient.
23. Check freezers, air conditioners and fire extinguishers for leaking CFCs.
24. Fix all of the leaky taps in the school.
25. Stop using helium balloons at fairs and celebrations. Each year they turn up in everything from birds' nests to the stomachs of turtles and whales.

Index